Other Books by John Crowley

NOVELTY

John Crowley

A Foundation Book

DOUBLEDAY

New York London Toronto Sydney Auckland

NOVELTY

Published by Doubleday, a division of
Bantam Doubleday Dell Publishing Group, Inc.
666 Fifth Avenue, New York, New York 10103

Foundation, Doubleday, and the portrayal of the letter
F, are trademarks of Doubleday,
a division of Bantam Doubleday Dell Publishing
Group, Inc.

Library of Congress Cataloging-in-Publication Data

Crowley, John.
Novelty.
"A Foundation book."
I. Title.
PS3553.R597N6   1989   813'.54   88-31099
ISBN 0-385-26171-3 HB.
ISBN 0-385-26347-3 PB.

BOOK DESIGN BY CAROL A. MALCOLM

Contents

NOVELTY

THE NIGHTINGALE

SINGS AT NIGHT

The Nightingale
Sings at Night

THE NIGHTINGALE IS CALLED A NIGHTINGALE BE-
cause it sings at night.

There are other birds who cry in the night: the
whippoorwill complains and the owl hoots, the loon screams
and the nightjar calls. But the Nightingale is the only one who
sings: as beautifully as the lark sings in the morning and the
thrush at evening, the Nightingale sings at night.

But the Nightingale didn't always sing at night.

There was a time, long after the beginning of the world
but still a very long time ago, when the Nightingale sang only
in the day, and slept all night—like the blackbird and the wren
and the lark.

Each morning in those days, when night had fled away
and the earth tilted its face again into the sun, the Nightingale
awoke from sleep, along with the lark and the robin and the
wren. He drew his beak out from the feathers of his shoulder,
he fluffed out his brown plumage, and—as the long bars of
morning sun found their way into the thicket where he liked to
live—he sang.

In those days every morning seemed to be the first morning that ever was; everything the Nightingale saw, the green

leaves sparkling with dew, the multicolored morning sky, the mossy earth teeming with insects, the tall trees, the birds and beasts awakening, all seemed to have just been made that morning.

That was because Time had not yet been invented. But it was about to be invented.

On a certain morning very much like every other morning that had ever been, the Nightingale awoke and sang. As he sang, he saw someone coming through the glades of the forest where he lived. It was someone the Nightingale knew well, someone he loved, someone who caused him to sing even a longer and more beautiful song as she came closer.

There was no one in the whole world at all like her, and yet she was just a little like everything there is.

She had no name, in those days, this someone; for that matter, neither did anyone or anything else, because names hadn't been invented yet. But long after this story, she would come to be called Dame Kind.

The forest where she walked was all Dame Kind's work. She had planted the trees and the flowers in all their variety and helped them to grow. She had watered them with the rain and had set the sun to shine on them. It was she who had thought of filling the trees with birds and the air with insects and the rivers and the seas with fish and the earth with animals.

It was she who had thought of making the earth round, like a green and blue and white marble, and who set it turning in the sun, so that there would be day and night.

In fact, there was nothing on earth or in the sky that Dame Kind had not thought of and set in place and made to go. Every small difference there is between one thing and another, Dame Kind had first thought of. It was all her work, and she went about in it endlessly, fixing and changing and pruning and thinking of new things all the time.

It was no wonder that the Nightingale was glad to see her, and sang for her, because she had herself thought up the Nightingale, and thought up his song, too.

"Good morning," sang the Nightingale.

"It's a beautiful morning," Dame Kind said, and it was. She smiled, and the beauty of the morning was her smile. "And I," said Dame Kind, "have had a new idea."

"I bet it's a good one," said the Nightingale, who had never had an idea in all his life, good or bad.

"I *think* it's a good one," said Dame Kind. She thought a moment. "I'm sure it's a good one. Anyway, I've had it, and so there it is. Once you have an idea, there's no going back."

"If you say so," the Nightingale said cheerfully. "What is the new idea?"

"Well," Dame Kind said, "you can come see, if you like."

Together they went through the forest to the place where the new idea could be seen. In Dame Kind's footsteps as she walked there sprang up two new kinds of turtle, the speckles on the eggs that plovers lay, and the world's first June bug. The Nightingale didn't marvel at these things, because such things always happened where Dame Kind walked in the world.

At a certain place in the forest where the sun fell in patterns of light and dark on the flowers and the ferns, there sat a creature the Nightingale had never seen before.

"Is it the new idea?" asked the Nightingale.

"It is," said Dame Kind.

The creature had a round, flat face, and it stood on two legs, not four. Like some animals' babies, it was all naked, except on the top of its head, where long fur grew thickly. The sheen of its skin was soft and fragile-looking. There was something in its child's naked face, in its wondering eyes, that the Nightingale had never seen before in the faces of any of the

5

thousands upon thousands of creatures that Dame Kind had thought of.

For just a moment, watching the new creature, the Nightingale knew that the world was turning beneath him, turning and turning and never quite coming back to the same place.

"What is it?" the Nightingale whispered.

"It's a Girl," Dame Kind answered. "And here is a Boy to go with her."

Another creature came from the woods. The two seemed very much alike, though there were differences. The Boy had caught a crimson salamander, and he brought it to show the Girl.

The Nightingale didn't understand. "Boy? Girl?"

"Those are their names," said Dame Kind.

"Names?"

"They thought them up themselves," Dame Kind said proudly. "With a little help from me."

The Nightingale marveled now. Never in all the forest had he ever heard of a creature that thought things up. He himself had never thought up anything. "How does it happen that they thought up names?" he asked.

"Well," Dame Kind said, going into the forest glade where the Boy and the Girl sat together, "that's the new idea."

From a distance—he didn't yet like to get too close to the new idea—the Nightingale watched the Boy and the Girl playing with the salamander the Boy had caught. What clever hands they had! Gently and quickly their flexible long fingers turned this way and that, picking up the salamander and putting it down, prodding it, caging it and releasing it. The Girl freed it at last, and then, as though her hands could not be at rest, she picked up something else—a flower, by the stem, between thumb and finger.

When they saw Dame Kind, the two new creatures ran to

her, smiling and bringing her the flowers they had gathered. She sat with them, and they climbed into her lap, and she hugged them to her bosom, and they laughed and talked with her about all the things they had seen in the world since they had come to be.

"Look!" said the Girl, pointing up to the sky, from which a flood of hot golden light fell, warming her face.

"Yes," Dame Kind said. "It's lovely and warm."

"We call it the Sun," the Boy said.

"That's a good name," said Dame Kind fondly.

The Nightingale watched them for a time, and then, still marveling, he flew off to attend to the business of his life: to eat bugs and berries, to sing in the sun, and raise his young.

"Well," he said to himself, "it certainly is a wonderful new idea.

"I'm sure *I* never would have thought of it."

Dame Kind walked in the forest with the Boy and the Girl, holding a hand of each, and telling them about the world that she had made.

She told them what things were good to eat and what were not, and the difference seemed very clear to the Boy and the Girl, as though they had always known it.

She told them of some things they should take care about. She said they shouldn't kick open hornets' nests, or jump off high places, or get in fights with large fierce animals.

The children laughed, because they knew all these things very well, from the very first moment they came to be.

At evening they came to the edges of the forest, to an open place where the darkening sky was broad and high and deep and far away, and trimmed with colored cloud.

"What's beyond there?" asked the Boy, pointing far off.

"More of the world," said Dame Kind.

"As nice as this?" asked the Girl.

"Much the same," said Dame Kind.

"What are those lights?" asked the Boy, pointing up.

"They are far, far away," Dame Kind said. "So far that no amount of traveling could bring you much closer to them. They are huger than you can imagine, and there are more of them than you will ever know. They stitch the sky together, and without them nothing would be at all."

"I'll call them Stars," said the Boy.

"Oh," said the Girl, looking to the east. "Oh, look, what's that?"

Over the far purple hills there had arisen a sliver of golden light. As the Boy and the Girl watched, it grew larger, lifting itself slowly above the earth.

"Oh, how beautiful," said the Girl. "What is it?"

The golden light grew round as it rose. It pulled itself free of the purple hills and rolled into the sky. It was huge, and bright, and looked down on the Boy and the Girl with a wise expression on its round, fat face.

"It comes and goes," said Dame Kind. "It's lovely to look at, but not as important as it thinks. It steals its light from the Sun, when the Sun's back is turned."

"I'll call it the Moon," said the Girl.

"I wonder," said Dame Kind, "why you think everything in the world should have a name."

Dame Kind had made the Moon, of course, just as she had made everything the Boy and the Girl saw and named.

But she couldn't remember just then *why* she had made it.

I must have had a reason, she thought, looking up into the big fat face that looked down. The smile on the face of the Moon seemed to say: *I know the reason.*

Dame Kind felt troubled. She took the Boy's hand and the Girl's hand and led them back into the forest. "Dear children," she said. "You are my wonderful new idea, and I love you very much.

"I've shown you everything in my world that can give you joy and pleasure, and I've explained about some of the inconveniences there are, and how to avoid them.

"I've made you as well as I could to fit into this world I have made, and I will always think about your happiness, just as I do about the happiness of every other creature that is.

"Now I want to tell you something.

"For your own happiness, don't talk too much with . . ." She gestured over her shoulder with her thumb.

"The Moon," said the Girl.

"The Moon," said the Boy.

"The Moon," said Dame Kind. "I think it's not to be trusted. I forget just now why I think so, but I do. It comes and goes, and steals its light from the Sun, and it's not to be trusted.

"Will you do that?"

"If you say so," said the Girl.

"If you say so," said the Boy, and yawned a huge yawn.

"Good," said Dame Kind. "You are wonderful children, and I'm sure you'll be happy. We won't mention it again.

"Now I'll leave you, because I have a thousand thousand other things to see to. But I'll always be near, and I'll always have you in my thoughts.

"No matter what."

Dame Kind kissed them both, and then she went away, to pour rain, to plant seeds, to turn the world in its socket. She had some new ideas for beetles; as anybody who has ever looked closely at the world knows, Dame Kind is very fond of beetles.

The Boy and the Girl lay down to sleep on the soft blooming moss of the forest floor. There was nothing to trouble them, and nothing to alarm them. When they slept, they had no dreams, because dreams had not been invented yet.

Before she slept, the Girl looked up once at the Moon.

It had grown smaller as it went higher in the sky, and it had lost its golden color; its stolen light was white and cold. The light crept through the branches of the trees and stole over the flowers and the ferns, making them all black and silver. It was beautiful and strange, and the face of the Moon looked down into the Girl's face and smiled a far-off smile, as though it knew something about the Girl that the Girl herself did not know.

The Girl turned away then, and put her arm around the Boy, and closed her eyes, and slept.

The days came and went, each one so much like the last that it was hard to tell whether it was the same day happening over and over again, or new days coming to replace old ones.

The Boy and the Girl ate when they were hungry and drank when they were thirsty; when they were sleepy, they slept.

With their quick feet and clever fingers they explored the world Dame Kind had made, giving a name to everything that seemed to have something different about it.

One leaf of a tree seemed to be pretty much the same as every other leaf, so they didn't give a separate name to each leaf; they called them all Leaves.

There was not *much* difference between a Bat and a Bird, but there was a difference; so they called one a Bat and the other a Bird.

The difference between Day and Night was the biggest difference they knew. In the Day the sun shone and there was light; then they went exploring, and gave names to things, and ate and drank. In the Night there was no light, and they lay on the mossy floor of the forest and put their arms around one another and slept.

And while they slept, the Moon came and went, rolling over the dark-blue sky and looking down on them.

There was a night when, very close to where the Boy and the Girl lay asleep, an owl hooted, and the Girl awoke.

She looked around her in the sparkling dimness. The fireflies had put out their lights. But there was a faint silvery light on the leaves and flowers.

She looked overhead.

Through the branches of the trees, on the deep-blue surface of the night sky, surrounded by the far-off stars, the Moon looked down on her.

But it was not the same Moon.

The Moon she had once seen was a round, fat face, with a smile that puffed out its cheeks, and heavy-lidded eyes half closed.

This Moon was a thin crescent of light, with a shape like a fingernail paring; it had a thin, thin face that looked away, and a small pursed mouth, and a cold, cold eye that glanced sidewise at the Girl.

"Are you the Moon?" she asked.

"I am," said the Moon, "I am."

"What became of the other Moon?" asked the Girl.

"What other Moon is that?" the Moon asked back. Its voice was as cold and far-off as its light, but the Girl could hear it clearly.

"You aren't the same," said the Girl.

"Is that so?" said the Moon. "Well, there it is."

"Why?"

"Oh, well," the Moon said, and looked away. "That's my secret."

"Did you change?" asked the Girl.

"That would be telling," said the Moon.

The Girl lay watching the Moon a long time, trying to think of a question she could ask that would make the Moon tell what it knew. It bothered her that the Moon had a secret she could not guess.

"There must be more than one Moon," she said. "That's all."

The Moon said: "Is that what you think?"

"It must be," said the Girl.

"Hm," said the Moon, and smiled a secret smile. It had rolled on by now, rolling toward the west; and without saying another word, it rolled behind the trees where the Girl could see it no more.

In the morning she told the Boy: "We have to give the Moon a different name."

"Why?" asked the Boy.

"Because it's different now," the Girl said. "I saw it last night. Once it was fat and round. Now it's thin and sharp, and looks away. That's a difference. And different things should have different names."

The Boy couldn't think of an answer to this. He didn't like the Moon, and didn't like to think about it. "Maybe it wasn't the Moon at all," he said.

"It was," the Girl said. "I asked."

The Boy said: "We weren't supposed to talk to the Moon! Don't you remember?"

"We weren't supposed to talk to the Moon too much," the Girl said. "I didn't talk too much."

The Boy turned away. He had a feeling within him that he had never felt before in all the time he had been in the world. He didn't know what it was, and he didn't know why he felt it. "The Moon is the Moon," he said. "It doesn't change, and it has only one name. Two names would just be confusing. And we're not supposed to talk with it."

He sat without turning around until the Girl said: "I won't talk with it again."

And so she didn't. But she thought about it.

It's a strange thing about names: when you know the name of something, you can think about it even when the thing itself isn't there before your face.

Even though the Girl took care not to look up at the Moon's smile, she could think about the Moon, and about whether it was one Moon or two. She could do that because she had a name to think of.

She could say to herself: "The Moon," and even though the sun was shining and making patterns of dark and light on the flowers and the ferns of the forest, she could see the cold, white, narrow face of the Moon and feel its silver light, and ask it questions that it would not answer.

The Boy learned this strange thing about names, too.

He found that he could sit and think about things that were not there before his face.

He could say to himself, "a Squirrel," and the squirrel he had thought of would run around his mind, and pick up nuts in its little black hands, and eat them in its quick squirrel way.

He could say to himself, "a Stone," and there would be a stone: not any particular stone, just a stone; a stone that was something like all the stones he had ever seen but not exactly like any one.

And, most interesting of all, he could think of the stone and the squirrel at the same time, and think about the many differences between them.

One afternoon the Nightingale came upon him while he was busy with this, thinking of the names of things, putting them together, and thinking about the difference between them.

What the Nightingale saw was this: he saw the Boy put

13

his cheek in his hand and rest his elbow on his knee. He saw the Boy's lips move, but no sound came out. Then he saw the Boy cross his legs a different way and rest his chin on his fist. He saw the Boy scratch his head, and laugh at nothing, and get up and throw himself down on the ground, and pillow his hands under his head.

The Nightingale didn't know what the Boy was doing, and he grew curious.

"Hello there," he sang from a branch above the Boy's head.

"Hello, Bird," said the Boy, looking up and smiling.

"What is it that you're doing there?" the Nightingale asked.

"I was just thinking," said the Boy.

"Oh," said the Nightingale. "Thinking?"

"Just thinking," said the Boy.

"Oh," said the Nightingale. "What were you thinking up? Names?"

"I wasn't thinking anything *up,*" said the Boy. "Not just now. I was just thinking."

"Hm," said the Nightingale, and he sang a few notes, because he had nothing to say.

"I was thinking of a question," said the Boy.

"That's clever of you," said the Nightingale.

The Boy crossed his legs a different way. "The question is this: Why is there anything at all, and not nothing?"

The Nightingale marveled at the Boy. "That's a good question," he said. "I never would have thought of it."

"But what's the answer?" asked the Boy.

"Answer?" said the Nightingale.

"A question has to have an answer."

"Does it?" said the Nightingale.

"Oh, forget it," said the Boy.

"All right," said the Nightingale, and he sang a long song.

The Boy listened to the song. He thought: Why is there anything at all, and not nothing instead? Why should there be something, instead of nothing at all? The question went on and on inside his head, and made him feel strange. The more he thought about it the stranger he felt: as though he himself did not exist.

This was the first time anyone had ever thought of this question, and from that day to this no one has ever thought of an answer: Why is there anything at all, and not nothing?

While the Nightingale sang and the Boy thought, the Girl, walking on the edges of the forest, discovered a strange thing.

The Moon was shining in the day.

The sun had set, but it was still coloring the sky in the west. And above the green hills the Moon had risen.

It was fatter, and smiling once again, as it had been when Dame Kind had first shown it to them. It seemed to be not quite all there, though. It was faint and very pale, and the Girl could partly see through it: she could see blue sky through its white skin.

"Hello again," said the Moon.

"Hello," said the Girl. She had forgotten, in her wonder, that she had promised not to talk with the Moon. "You've changed again."

"Is that so?" said the Moon. Its voice was fainter and farther away than ever.

"Unless," the Girl said, "there are three Moons: one fat one, one thin one, and one that shines in the day. Is that the answer?"

"What's the question?" asked the Moon.

The Girl couldn't think just what the question was. She sat down and looked up at the Moon. She thought: I am the question. For a long time she only sat and looked up, thinking: I am the question. But she could not think how to ask it.

Now a star or two was shining. The blue of the sky was

darkening. And the Moon was growing brighter, more solid, more like itself.

"I'll tell you this," it said, rolling higher into the sky and smiling more broadly. "You and I are alike."

"We are?" said the Girl.

"Oh, very much alike," the Moon said.

"How are we alike?" asked the Girl.

"Would you like to know?" said the Moon. "Then you keep your eye on me."

Now the night was deep. Around the edges of the sky the stars were numberless; but in the center the Moon was bright and put out the stars. Its silver light coated the world with strangeness. "I am strong," the Moon said, "and so are you; but we're more alike than that. You are beautiful, and so am I; but we're more alike than that."

"How are we alike?" the Girl asked. "Tell me."

"Oh, you'll see," the Moon said. "Watch me come and go, and you'll see. You'll see it's true."

The Girl, sitting in the stream of the Moon's light, and hearing its voice, knew that the Moon was right. She grew afraid. She said: "We weren't supposed to talk to you."

"Oh?" said the Moon. "Who told you so?"

"She," the Girl said, even more afraid. "She told us so. She who made us both."

"Oho," the Moon said. "I wonder why she said that."

"I don't know," the Girl said.

"I wonder," said the Moon. "Do you think—perhaps— that there is something that I know, something she wants you not to find out?"

"I don't know," said the Girl.

"I wonder," said the Moon.

"She told us everything," said the Girl.

"Did she," said the Moon. "Did she, now."

"What is it that you know?" asked the Girl.

"You'll find out," said the Moon. "Just keep your eye on me."

At that moment the Moon looked away. Its silver smile faded. Clouds, dark as slate and edged with lacy white, raced over the sky and across the face of the Moon.

Far away, there was a sound of thunder.

The thunder said: "What's going on?"

The Moon grew small, and it sped through the racing clouds as though it were being chased. The stars went out. The Girl hugged herself, feeling a cold wind blow.

The wind said: "If I were you, I wouldn't talk with the Moon."

The Girl saw the Moon swallowed up in black clouds. She heard it say, as it went away: "Just keep your eye on me."

"If I were you," Dame Kind said (for it was her voice in the thunder, and her voice in the wind), "I wouldn't listen to the Moon."

The Girl was afraid, but she said: "Why?"

Dame Kind sat down with her. "Dear child," she said. "Do you think I don't know best? I know how you're made, every little bit of you, every hair on your head! Didn't I make you myself, and didn't I make you just as you are so that you could be happy in the world I made, and give me joy in your happiness? And don't you think then that I know what's best for you?"

"But why?" the Girl asked again.

Dame Kind arose; she stamped her foot with a long roll of thunder, and she said in a loud voice: "Because I said so!"

She turned from the Girl and went away; and the rain fell in big, cold drops, pattering in the leaves of the trees and causing the birds and the animals to run and hide.

Dame Kind was puzzled and sad. Never before in all the world she had made, in all the time she had gone about in it, had she ever lost her temper and said: "Because I said so!"

But then, never before in all the world had anyone ever asked Dame Kind the question that the Girl had asked: "Why?"

The Girl said to the Boy: "The Moon does change."

"It does?" said the Boy. They were sitting in a little cave they had found, out of the rain that fell from leaf to leaf. "How do you know?"

"I saw it again," said the Girl. "And it was fat and big, not thin and sharp."

"Maybe," said the Boy, "there are three Moons."

"No," said the Girl. "It's one Moon, but it changes."

"I don't care," said the Boy. He still didn't like hearing the Girl talk about the Moon.

"The Moon," she said to him—softly, so that no one else would hear—"the Moon has a secret."

"How do you know?"

"Because it told me," said the Girl.

"We aren't supposed to talk to the Moon," said the Boy.

The Girl only took the Boy's hand, and waited. The rain fell and fell, like tears. And at last the Boy said: "What is the Moon's secret?"

"I don't know," said the Girl. "It won't tell. But it said: Keep your eye on me, and you'll see."

"It's probably not important," said the Boy. "It's something good to eat, or something to keep away from; or it's the name of something we haven't named yet."

"No," said the Girl. "It's not anything like that. It's something we don't know, and something we couldn't think of."

The Boy said: *"She* would know what it was." He pointed outward at the rainy world. "We'll ask *her.*"

"No," said the Girl. "She told us not to talk to the Moon. She doesn't want us to learn the Moon's secret."

"Why?" asked the Boy.

"I don't know," said the Girl.

The Boy wondered what the secret could be. He thought it *might* be the answer to the hard question he had thought of: *Why is there anything at all, and not nothing?*

If he could make the Moon tell him the answer to that question, he would know everything. But he didn't say this to the Girl.

He said: "Maybe, if we knew the Moon's secret, we would know as much as *she* does."

"Maybe," said the Girl.

"And then we could do the things that she does."

"Maybe," said the Girl. But she didn't think this was the Moon's secret. She thought that the Moon's secret was a secret about herself: something she didn't know about herself, that the Moon knew.

But she didn't say this to the Boy.

She said: "We *can* learn what the secret is. We must."

"How?" said the Boy.

"We'll do as it said," the Girl answered. "We'll keep our eyes on it, and learn."

The Boy's heart, for some reason, or for no reason at all, had begun to beat hard and fast. "All right," he said. "We'll keep our eyes on it, and see."

And so they did.

They watched that night, and the next night, and every night from then on.

They watched the Moon change: each night it arose at a different time, and each night it grew thinner. Its fat face was worn away on one side, till it was like a melon cut in half. Its smile grew strange and its eyes were sad.

"Time eats me," said the Moon to the Boy.

"What is Time?" asked the Boy.

"You don't know?" said the Moon. "Then watch me, and learn."

The next night the Moon was thinner, and the next night, thinner still. Now it had become the thin, sharp-faced Moon that looked away.

"The Moon does change," the Boy said. "Once it was one way, and now it's another way. On one night it's fat, and then it grows thinner. Last night is different from tonight. Tomorrow night will be different again."

"Different things should have different names," said the Girl.

The difference between the way things once were, and the way things are now, and the way things will be, was the biggest difference the Boy and the Girl had yet learned.

They called the difference Time.

"Is that the Moon's secret?" asked the Boy.

The Girl asked the Moon: "Is that your secret?"

But the Moon only answered: "Keep your eye on me."

And still the Moon grew thinner with every night that passed. Now it was only the palest and thinnest of fingernail parings, and almost not there at all.

"I die," said the Moon.

"What does that mean?" asked the Boy.

"Just watch me," said the Moon, and it seemed that a silver tear stood in its eye. "Good-bye," it said.

And the next night there was no Moon at all.

The stars glowed more brightly than they ever had, but the night was deeply dark. The Boy and the Girl could hardly see each other.

"It's gone," said the Boy. "Once it was, and now it's not anymore. Once there was a Moon, and now there's not a Moon anymore. It dies." And he sat very close to the Girl in the fearful darkness. "That's the Moon's secret," he said.

The next night was just as dark.

But on the next night, as the Boy and the Girl sat close together watching the darkening sky in the east, they saw, rising over the purple hills, as thin as could be and as pale as anything, a new Moon.

"Moon!" said the Girl in wonder. "You came back!"

"Did I?" said the new Moon. Now it faced the opposite way, and its small cold voice was smaller and colder than before. "Well, I come and I go. Ah, but it's good to be young!"

And every night thereafter as they watched, the new Moon grew fatter and fuller. Its smile broadened and its cheeks puffed out. "Ah," he said proudly to the Girl, "it's good to be strong and beautiful."

"Am I like you?" asked the Girl. "Am I strong and beautiful?"

"You're very much like me," said the Moon. "Look inside yourself and see."

The nights passed. The full-faced new Moon began to shrink and lose its shape, just as the old Moon had done.

"I wane," said the Moon. "I grow old."

"Will I grow old?" the Girl asked.

"We're alike," the Moon said. "Look inside yourself and see."

The Girl looked within herself. And she saw that what the Moon said was true: they were alike. She too would change. She was changing even now, as though she had a Moon of her own within her. She was strong and young and beautiful: and yet she too would grow old. "That's the Moon's secret," she said. She had thought that the Moon's secret was a secret about herself: and she was right.

When day came, the Boy and the Girl looked around themselves. The world seemed to be different from the way it had been.

"Everything's changed," said the Girl. She looked at the Boy. "You've changed."

"You've changed," said the Boy, looking at the Girl. "Why?"

"We're different now," said the Girl. "Different things should have different names."

"Why have we changed?" asked the Boy.

"Well," said the Girl, as the Moon had said to her, "there it is."

"What name will you have, then?" the Boy asked.

"I will be the Woman."

He straightened his shoulders, he lifted his chin, and he looked firmly far off. "All right," he said. "Then I'll be the Man."

They took hands then, and looked at each other, and felt suddenly shy, and didn't know what to do next.

The Man and the Woman walked together in the forest. They saw that the summer's flowers had wilted and drooped on their brown stems. They hadn't noticed that before.

They saw a hunting hawk fall from the sky on a brown mouse, and they heard a tiny shriek as the mouse was speared by the hawk's sharp claws.

They saw a frog on a lily pad shoot out its long tongue, catch a careless dragonfly, and eat it. And they saw a heron step up silently on long legs behind the frog, catch it in its beak, and swallow it.

They kicked the dry brown leaves underfoot, leaves that had once danced green and dewy on the branches of the trees.

"Everything's changed," the Woman said.

"Nothing lasts," the Man said. He took the Woman's hand in his. "For everything, there was a time before it was alive, and a time after it isn't alive anymore."

Bigger than the difference between a squirrel and a stone, bigger than the difference between night and day, was the difference between being alive and not being alive anymore.

They called the difference Death.

"I die," said the Moon to the Woman that night. It had grown as thin as thin, and was almost not there.

"Will I die?" asked the Woman, and the Moon didn't answer; but she needed only to look inside herself to know.

She looked up, and blinked the tears away that had come into her eyes. "Oh, look!" she said. "Look, look!"

For she could see, as the old Moon rolled away, that held within its long, long arms was the new Moon that would come to be in its place. It wasn't easy to see the new Moon; it was a pale, ghostly shadow. But it was like a promise. And the Woman knew that the promise had been made to her: for she and the Moon were alike.

"Now I know the Moon's secret," she said to herself, though what she knew she could never say in words.

Now through all this time the Nightingale had gone on with the business of his life: that is, singing in the day and sleeping at night, eating bugs and berries, raising his young and going about in the world to see what he could see.

One day was very much like another, as it had always been and would always be.

He didn't know that the Man and the Woman had invented Time.

When he came upon them one day, he greeted them as usual: "Hello, Boy," he sang. "Hello, Girl."

"I'm not a boy," the Man said. "Not anymore. Once I was, but now I'm a Man."

"I'm not a girl," said the Woman. "I've changed. Now I'm a Woman."

"Oh," said the Nightingale. "Sorry. I'll try to remember." He sang a few notes, and then he said to the Man: "Did you ever find an answer to your question?"

"No," said the Man. "But I learned a lot of things."

"Is that so," said the Nightingale.

"Yes," said the Man. He pointed up at the Nightingale. "Things aren't as you think they are."

"No?" said the Nightingale.

"No," said the Man. "Listen to the Moon. You'll learn."

"Oh?" said the Nightingale. "The Moon never spoke to *me*. What did the Moon say?"

"There is Time," said the Man. He came closer to the branch where the Nightingale sat. "There was a time before you were," he said, "and there will be a time after. You won't live forever. You will die."

"Do you think so?" said the Nightingale, who didn't know at all what the Man meant.

"You will. There are hawks, Bird. There are foxes. There are owls and weasels."

"But not just now," said the Nightingale, looking around quickly.

"There will be!" said the Man. His expression was so fierce and strange that the Nightingale flew to a higher branch away from him.

"You will die, Bird!" said the man in a terrible voice. "You will die!"

The Nightingale was astonished and troubled and didn't know what to do. So he sang. "It's all right," he sang. "It's all right."

"It's not all right!" cried the Man. "It's not. Because you'll die. And so will I!"

And just at that moment, with a noise of winds and many rivers, with a clamor of birdsong and a sound of leaves falling, Dame Kind came striding through the forest toward them.

The Woman leapt up. "We'll run and hide!" she said. She took the Man's hand. "Quick, we must!" she said, and together they ran to hide in the forest.

"Come out," said Dame Kind.

She waited.

"Come out," she said again. And the Man and the Woman came out from where they had hidden themselves.

"Why did you hide?" asked Dame Kind.

"Because we were afraid," said the Woman.

Dame Kind looked at them sadly for a long time. Then she said in a gentle voice: "Who told you you should be afraid?"

The Man and the Woman looked away from Dame Kind, and they made no answer.

"And who told you that you would die?" Dame Kind asked them. "Was it the Moon?"

"It was the Moon," said the Man.

"No," said the Woman, and she raised her eyes to Dame Kind. "It wasn't the Moon. We learned it ourselves."

And that was true.

Dame Kind took the Man's shoulder in her great hand. She gently brushed away the hair that fell before the Woman's face. She said, "Oh, dear. Oh, my poor children." Then she covered her eyes with her hand and shook her head. "Oh, my," she said. "Oh, dear."

"We only wanted to learn," said the Man. "There *is* Time, and there *is* Change, and there *is* Death. And you never told us."

"You never told us," the Woman said, her eyes filling with tears. "You never told us we would die."

Dame Kind lowered her hand from her eyes. "No," she said. "I didn't. And I will tell you why. Until you thought of those things, they did not exist.

"Until you thought of Time, there was no such thing.

Things went on as they always had; there wasn't a Yesterday, and there wasn't a Tomorrow; there was only Today.

"Until you thought of Change, everything remained the same. The flowers were always growing, the young ones were always being born, the sun and the stars and yes, even the Moon, were always doing just as they always do. Now you will see them change, you alone, and nothing will ever be quite the same for you.

"Until you thought of Death, dear children, nothing died. My creatures only lived. They didn't know of a time when they had not been, and they couldn't think of a time when they would not be. And so they lived forever. And so would you have too: except that you thought of Death.

"And when you thought of those things," she said, "you thought of fear, too.

"And you thought of weeping." She dried the Woman's eyes with the sleeve of her gown.

"And the worst thing is," Dame Kind said, and a tear came to her own eye, "that now you have thought of these things, you cannot take them back, ever. That's the way it is with ideas. Once you have one, there's no going back."

The Woman wept, and the Man hung his head at these words of Dame Kind's; and the Nightingale remembered a morning—an important morning—when Dame Kind had said those very words to him: Once you have an idea, there's no going back.

Dame Kind crossed her arms and rose up to her full height. "And now," she said. She shrugged her shoulders. "Well, what now? I just don't know. I don't know if you can ever be happy here again; not as happy as you once were." She looked around her at the blooming forest. "I can't have you going about the world weeping. I can't have you telling the birds and the beasts that they will die. I can't have that."

"It's all right," sang the Nightingale. He hadn't understood much of what had passed between Dame Kind and the Man and the Woman, but he didn't like to see them sad. "It's all right," he sang. "I don't mind."

"All right then," said the Man. His face was brave, and his eyes were dry. His knees shook, but he pretended that they didn't. "All right then, we'll go someplace else." He clenched his fists and set his jaw. "If we can't be happy here, we'll go someplace else."

"You can't," Dame Kind said. "There isn't anyplace else."

The Man put his arm around the Woman. "All right," he said, "all right then: I'll make one up. I'll make up another place. I'll make up another place, a better place, and go there."

"Oh, dear," said Dame Kind. She lifted her fingers to her chin in alarm and puzzlement.

The Woman brushed the last of her tears from her eyes. She said, "Yes! I'll make up someplace else, too. A better place. And I'll go there."

"No!" the Man said, turning on her. "*I'll* make up another place, and we'll *both* go there. Come on!" And he took the Woman's arm and led her away; and though she looked back once, and though her eyes began again to fill with tears, she knew that she could not leave the Man; and so she went with him, and they went out of the forest together.

"Perhaps," Dame Kind said when they were gone, "perhaps I made a mistake." She sat sadly on the stump of a tree she had made long ago, and had made to fall down, too. "Perhaps the Boy and the Girl were a mistake."

"Oh, no," the Nightingale said. "I don't think you could make a mistake."

"I didn't think so either," Dame Kind said. "Well—I have

made one or two—some animals and plants that didn't work out—but they all came right in the end. They did their part."

"So will the Boy and the Girl."

"I don't know," said Dame Kind. "It's odd, having things come about in the world that I didn't think of. This place they're going to make up: What will it be like? I don't know. Because I didn't think of it."

"But you did," said the Nightingale. "I don't know anything about it, but—didn't you think up the Boy and the Girl? If you thought up the Boy and the Girl, didn't you think up everything they can think up? In a way, I mean."

Dame Kind thought about that.

"I guess I did," she said at last. A broad smile came over her face, a smile that was like the sun coming from clouds; and in fact at that very moment a mass of thick clouds did go away from the face of the sun, and the sun's smile remade the patterns of light and dark amid the ferns and the flowers. "I guess I did at that. In a way." She sighed, and stood. A thousand thousand duties were calling to her. "Anyway, I'll just have to get used to it. And I don't suppose the story's over yet."

The Nightingale didn't know what she meant by that, but he was glad to see Dame Kind happy again. He sang a few notes. "It's all right," he sang.

"You know," Dame Kind said to him as she went away, "all those things the Man said are true. About Time. About Death."

"It is?" said the Nightingale.

"But if I were you," said Dame Kind, "I wouldn't worry about it."

"If you say so," said the Nightingale, and his heart was filled with gladness.

And Dame Kind went away, to pour rain, to plant seeds, to turn the world in its socket. "And as for you," she said to the Moon when next she saw him, "from now on you will hold your tongue." She pinched its nose and squeezed its cheeks and locked up its lips until its face was hardly a face at all. "And from now on forever," she said, "when the Man and the Woman ask you questions, no matter how they insist, you will answer nothing, nothing, nothing at all."

And so it has been, from that day to this.

It was another day when the Nightingale saw the Man again, but whether it was the next day, or the day after that, or many many days later, the Nightingale didn't know, for he didn't keep track of such things.

The Nightingale was singing in the forest when he saw the Man some way off.

The Man stood looking into the forest where the sun fell in patterns of dark and light on the flowers and the ferns.

"Why don't you come in?" said the Nightingale. "Come in and rest, and have a chat."

"I can't," the Man said. "I can't pass through this gate."

"What gate is that?" the Nightingale asked.

"This one here," the Man said, pointing ahead of him with the stick he carried.

But the Nightingale could see no gate there. "Well, I don't know what you mean," he said, "but if you say so."

The Man went on staring into the forest, through the gate that he alone saw there. He seemed at once sad and angry and resolute. The Nightingale sang a few notes and said, "Tell me. How is it with you now? How did the place you made up turn out? Is it better than here?"

The Man sat down, holding his stick in his lap, and put his elbows on his knees and his cheeks in his hands.

"I wouldn't say *better,"* he said a little sadly. "It's interesting. Bigger. I think it's bigger, but we haven't gone very far yet. There's a lot of work to do."

"A lot of what?" asked the Nightingale.

"Work," the Man said, looking up at the branch where the Nightingale sat and saying the word a little bitterly. "Work. You wouldn't understand."

"I think," the Nightingale said cheerfully, "I think I understand you less and less. But don't hold it against me."

The Man laughed, and shook his head. "No, I won't," he said. He sighed. "It'll be all right. It's the nights that are the hardest time."

"Why is that?" asked the Nightingale. He hardly knew what Night was, after all; he slept all through it, and when he awoke, it was gone.

"Well, there are *Things* in the dark. Or anyway I *think* there are Things. I can't be sure. *She* says they're Dreams."

"Dreams?"

"Things that you think are there but aren't."

"If you say so," said the Nightingale.

"But it doesn't matter," said the Man. He grasped the stick in the two clever hands the Nightingale had always marveled at. "See, I've got this stick now. If anything comes near—" He struck out with the stick, which made a swishing noise in the empty air.

"That's a good idea," said the Nightingale. "I never would have thought of it."

The Man was turning the stick in his hands with a dissatisfied expression. "I could make it better," he said. "Somehow better. Stronger. Like stone—that's the strongest thing. So it would cut, like a sharp stone." He made an imaginary jab with the stick, like a jay's sharp beak breaking into an egg, except there was no egg there. Then he put down the stick and sat again with his cheeks in his hands.

"Anyway," the Man said, "there's nothing to be afraid of *now.*"

"No," said the Nightingale.

"But *then,*" the Man said. "Soon. There might be something to be afraid of."

"If you say so," said the Nightingale.

The Man rose to go, shouldering the stick he had thought of. "It'll be all right," he said again. "It's just the nights that are hard."

He looked back once through the gate that he saw there, which kept him from the precincts of the forest, and which the Nightingale couldn't see.

"Well, good-bye then," he sang. "Good-bye."

And the Man went away down the valley to the place he and the Woman had made up.

When darkness came that night, the Nightingale perched on his usual branch. He fluffed his feathers; he bent his legs so that his sharp, small feet locked themselves tightly around the branch (so that he wouldn't fall from the tree in his sleep). He nestled his beak in the feathers of his shoulder and closed his eyes.

But sleep wouldn't come.

The Nightingale's eyes opened. He shut them again, and again they opened.

The Nightingale was thinking.

For the first time in his life, and the first time in all the time there had been a Nightingale, the Nightingale was thinking about something that was not in front of his eyes.

He was thinking about the Man and the Woman, alone in the place they had made up, wherever it was.

He was thinking of what the Man had said to him: that it was all right, but that the nights were hard.

That there were Things in the night to be afraid of.

The Nightingale took his beak out from the feathers of his shoulder and looked around himself.

There were no Things in the night to be afraid of that he could see.

There was a sparkling dimness; there were the black shapes of the sleeping trees and the very, very dark pool of the forest floor. There was the secret Moon turning in the clouds and saying nothing. There were stars, and there were breezes. But no Things.

"It's all right," the Nightingale sang. And because there were no other songs being sung, the Nightingale's song was stronger and sweeter than he had ever heard it.

"It's all right," he sang again, and again his song floated out into the night, and lingered, all alone.

That's interesting, thought the Nightingale, *very interesting: but the night is for sleep.* He tucked his beak again into the feathers of his shoulder and closed his eyes.

Without even knowing he had done so, he found after a few moments that he had opened his eyes again and was looking around himself and thinking.

He was thinking, *What if I fly to where the Man and the Woman are?*

If they hear me sing, he thought, *they might not be so afraid. If they heard me singing, they would remember that day will come. And anyway,* he thought, *what's the use of sleeping all night, when you can be awake and singing?*

He made up his mind to do this, even though it was something he had never done before. He looked around himself, wondering how he would find the Man and the Woman. He unlocked his feet from the branch where he sat, opened his brown wings, and sailed off carefully into the cool darkness.

He flew, not knowing exactly where he should fly; now and then he stopped to rest, and to eat a few of the bugs that were so plentiful, and to look at the new world of night he had discovered, and to test his song against it. And after a time that seemed to him more short than long, he came upon the place where the Man and the Woman were.

"Why, it isn't very far away at all," he said to himself. "In fact it seems just like the same old forest to me."

There was one difference, though.

In the place where the Man and the Woman were, there was something bright, something yellow and orange and red, dancing and shifting and shining. It was as though a tiny piece of the Sun had been broken off and set before them.

The Man and the Woman had thought of fire.

They sat before their fire, with their arms around each other, looking into the fire and into the deep darkness around them. In one hand the Man held the stick he had thought of.

The Nightingale didn't like to get too close to the new idea of fire, which was surely marvelous but a little scary; and so he hid himself in a thicket. And from there he sang.

"It's all right," he sang.

The Woman listened. "Did you hear that?" she asked.

"What?" said the Man, looking up in alarm.

"Listen," the Woman said.

The Nightingale sang: "It's all right."

The Man and the Woman listened to the song. In the stillness of the night it was so clear that it seemed they heard it for the first time. They had never noticed that it was so beautiful, so strong and soft, so happy and sad all at once.

"Once," said the Man, "he sang in the day."

"Now he sings at night," the Woman said.

"We'll call him the Nightingale," said the Man.

The Woman rested her head on the Man's shoulder. Hearing the Nightingale's song, she remembered the forest they had left. She remembered the happiness they had had there. She remembered the sun falling in patterns of light and darkness on the flowers and the ferns. She remembered it all, and hot tears came to her eyes, because they had lost it all.

33

"It's all right," sang the Nightingale.

The Woman thought: *I can remember it all.* And then she thought: *If I can remember it all, then I haven't lost it—not completely. If I can remember it, I will have it always, even if only a little bit of it. Always: no matter what.*

She closed her eyes. "It's all right," she said. "It will be all right. You'll see."

The Man put his arm around her, glad of her warmth in the darkness. He listened to the Nightingale sing, and he thought: *Day will come. No matter what happened before, day will always come. Tomorrow the sun will lift itself over the hills, and the world will be new. What will it be like?* He didn't know, but he thought it might be good. He hoped it would be good.

"It's all right," sang the Nightingale.

"It's all right," said the Man, and he held the Woman in his arms. "I think it will be all right." He closed his eyes, too. "Anyway," he said, "I don't think the story's over yet."

And so, from that day to this, the Nightingale has sung his song at night.

In the spring and summer, when his heart is full and the nights are soft and warm, he sings his song of hope and remembrance, his song that no one can imitate and no one can describe.

In the day, too, he can sometimes be heard singing, but so can the blackbird and the thrush and many other singers, and the Nightingale is hard to hear. But in the night he is alone: he is the only one who sings at night.

It was the only new idea the Nightingale had ever had, and he never had another one.

GREAT
WORK
OF
TIME

I: The Single
Excursion
of Caspar Last

I F WHAT I AM TO SET DOWN IS A CHRONICLE, THEN IT MUST
differ from any other chronicle whatever, for it begins, not
in one time or place, but everywhere at once—or perhaps
everywhen is the better word. It might be begun at any point
along the infinite, infinitely broken coastline of time.

It might even begin within the forest in the sea: huge trees
like American redwoods, with their roots in the black ben-
thos, and their leaves moving slowly in the blue currents
overhead. There it might end as well.

It might begin in 1893—or in 1983. Yes: it might be as
well to begin with Last, in an American sort of voice (for we
are all Americans now, aren't we?) Yes, Last shall be first: pale,
fattish Caspar Last, on excursion in the springtime of 1983 to a
far, far part of the Empire.

The tropical heat clothed Caspar Last like a suit as he
disembarked from the plane. It was nearly as claustrophobic
as the hours he had spent in the middle seat of a three-across,
economy-class pew between two other cut-rate, one-week-
excursion, plane-fare-and-hotel-room holiday-makers in
monstrous good spirits. Like them, Caspar had taken the ex-

cursion because it was the cheapest possible way to get to and from this equatorial backwater. Unlike them, he hadn't come to soak up sun and molasses-dark rum. He didn't intend to spend all his time at the beach, or even within the twentieth century.

It had come down, in the end, to a matter of money. Caspar Last had never had money, though he certainly hadn't lacked the means to make it; with any application he could have made good money as a consultant to any of a dozen research firms, but that would have required a certain subjection of his time and thought to others, and Caspar was incapable of that. It's often said that genius can live in happy disregard of material circumstances, dress in rags, not notice its nourishment, and serve only its own abstract imperatives. This was Caspar's case, except that he wasn't happy about it: he was bothered, bitter, and rageful at his poverty. Fame he cared nothing for, success was meaningless except when defined as the solution to abstract problems. A great fortune would have been burdensome and useless. All he wanted was a nice bit of change.

He had decided, therefore, to use his "time machine" once only, before it and the principles that animated it were destroyed, for good he hoped. (Caspar always thought of his "time machine" thus, with scare-quotes around it, since it was not really a machine, and Caspar did not believe in time.) He would use it, he decided, to make money. Somehow.

The one brief annihilation of "time" that Caspar intended to allow himself was in no sense a test run. He knew that his "machine" would function as predicted. If he hadn't needed the money, he wouldn't use it at all. As far as he was concerned, the principles once discovered, the task was completed; like a completed jigsaw puzzle, it had no further interest; there was really nothing to do with it except gloat over it briefly and then sweep all the pieces randomly back into the box.

It was a mark of Caspar's odd genius that figuring out a scheme with which to make money out of the past (which was the only "direction" his "machine" would take him) proved almost as hard, given the limitations of his process, as arriving at the process itself.

He had gone through all the standard wish-fulfillments and rejected them. He couldn't, armed with today's race results, return to yesterday and hit the daily double. For one thing it would take a couple of thousand in betting money to make it worth it, and Caspar didn't have a couple of thousand. More importantly, Caspar had calculated the results of his present self appearing at any point within the compass of his own biological existence, and those results made him shudder.

Similar difficulties attended any scheme that involved using money to make money. If he returned to 1940 and bought, say, two hundred shares of IBM for next to nothing: in the first place there would be the difficulty of leaving those shares somehow in escrow for his unborn self; there would be the problem of the alteration this growing fortune would have on the linear life he had actually lived; and where was he to acquire the five hundred dollars or whatever was needed in the currency of 1940? The same problem obtained if he wanted to return to 1623 and pick up a First Folio of Shakespeare, or to 1460 and a Gutenberg Bible: the cost of the currency he would need rose in relation to the antiquity, thus the rarity and value, of the object to be bought with it. There was also the problem of walking into a bookseller's and plunking down a First Folio he had just happened to stumble on while cleaning out the attic. In any case, Caspar doubted that anything as large as a book could be successfully transported "through time." He'd be lucky if he could go and return in his clothes.

Outside the airport, Caspar boarded a bus with his fellow excursionists, already hard at work with their cameras and index fingers as they rode through a sweltering lowland out of which concrete-block light industry was struggling to be born. The hotel in the capital was as he expected, shoddy-American and intermittently refrigerated. He ceased to notice it, forwent the complimentary rum concoction promised with his tour, and after asking that his case be put in the hotel safe —extra charge for that, he noted bitterly—he went immediately to the Hall of Records in the government complex. The collection of old survey maps of the city and environs were more extensive than he had hoped. He spent most of that day among them searching for a blank place on the 1856 map, a place as naked as possible of buildings, brush, water, and that remained thus through the years. He discovered one, visited it by unmuffled taxi, found it suitable. It would save him from the awful inconvenience of "arriving" in the "past" and finding himself inserted into some local's wattle-and-daub wall. Next morning, then, he would be "on his way." If he had believed in time, he would have said that the whole process would take less than a day's time.

Before settling on this present plan, Caspar had toyed with the idea of bringing back from the past something immaterial: some knowledge, some secret that would allow him to make himself rich in his own present. Ships have gone down with millions in bullion: he could learn exactly where. Captain Kidd's treasure. Inca gold. Archaeological rarities buried in China. Leaving aside the obvious physical difficulties of these schemes, he couldn't be sure that their location wouldn't shift in the centuries between his glimpse of them and his "real" life span; and even if he could be certain, no one else would have much reason to believe him, and he didn't have the wherewithal to raise expeditions himself. So all that was out.

He had a more general, theoretical problem to deal with. Of course the very presence of his eidolon in the past would alter, in however inconsequential a way, the succeeding history of the world. The comical paradoxes of shooting one's own grandfather and the like neither amused nor intrigued him, and the chance he took of altering the world he lived in out of all recognition was constantly present to him. Statistically, of course, the chance of this present plan of his altering anything significantly, except his own personal fortunes, was remote to a high power. But his scruples had caused him to reject anything such as, say, discovering the Koh-i-noor diamond before its historical discoverers. No: what he needed to abstract from the past was something immensely trivial, something common, something the past wouldn't miss but that the present held in the highest regard; something that would take the briefest possible time and the least irruption of himself into the past to acquire; something he could reasonably be believed to possess through simple historical chance; and something tiny enough to survive the cross-time "journey" on his person.

It had come to him quite suddenly—all his ideas did, as though handed to him—when he learned that his great-great-grandfather had been a commercial traveler in the tropics, and that in the attic of his mother's house (which Caspar had never had the wherewithal to move out of) some old journals and papers of his still moldered. They were, when he inspected them, completely without interest. But the dates were right.

Caspar had left a wake-up call at the desk for before dawn the next morning. There was some difficulty about getting his case out of the safe, and more difficulty about getting a substantial breakfast served at that hour (Caspar expected not to eat during his excursion), but he did arrive at his chosen site before the horrendous tropical dawn broke, and after paying the taxi, he had darkness enough left in which to make his preparations and change into his costume. The costume—a linen suit, a shirt, hat, boots—had cost him twenty dollars in rental from a theatrical costumer, and he could only hope it was accurate enough not to cause alarm in 1856. The last item he took from his case was the copper coin, which had cost him quite a bit, as he needed one unworn and of the proper date. He turned it in his fingers for a moment, thinking that if, unthinkably, his calculations were wrong and he didn't survive this journey, it would make an interesting obol for Charon.

Out of the unimaginable chaos of its interminable stochastic fiction, Time thrust only one unforeseen oddity on Caspar Last as he, or something like him, appeared beneath a plantain tree in 1856: he had grown a beard almost down to his waist. It was abominably hot.

The suburbs of the city had of course vanished. The road he stood by was a muddy track down which a cart was being driven by a tiny and close-faced Indian in calico. He followed the cart, and his costume boots were caked with mud when at last he came into the center of town, trying to appear nonchalant and to remember the layout of the city as he had studied it in the maps. He wanted to speak to no one if possible, and he did manage to find the post office without affecting, however minutely, the heterogeneous crowd of blacks, Indians, and Europeans in the filthy streets. Having absolutely no sense of humor and very little imagination other than the most rigidly abstract helped to keep him strictly about his business and not to faint, as another might have, with wonder and astonishment at his translation, the first, last, and only of its kind a man would ever make.

"I would like," he said to the mulatto inside the brass and mahogany cage, "an envelope, please."

"Of course, sir."

"How long will it take for a letter mailed now to arrive locally?"

"Within the city? It would arrive in the afternoon post."

"Very good."

Caspar went to a long, ink-stained table, and with one of the steel pens provided, he addressed the envelope to Georg von Humboldt Last, Esq., Grand Hotel, City, in the approximation of an antique round hand that he had been practicing for weeks. There was a moment's doubt as he tried to figure how to fold up and seal the cumbersome envelope, but he did it, and gave this empty missive to the incurious mulatto. He slipped his precious coin across the marble to him. For the only moment of his adventure, Caspar's heart beat fast as he watched the long, slow brown fingers affix a stamp, cancel and date it with a pen-stroke, and drop it into a brass slot like a hungry mouth behind him.

It only remained to check into the Grand Hotel, explain about his luggage's being on its way up from the port, and sit silent on the hotel terrace, growing faint with heat and hunger and expectation, until the afternoon post.

The one aspect of the process Caspar had never been able to decide about was whether his eidolon's residence in the fiction of the past would consume any "time" in the fiction of the present. It did. When, at evening, with the letter held tight in his hand and pressed to his bosom, Caspar reappeared beardless beneath the plantain tree in the traffic-tormented and smoky suburb, the gaseous red sun was squatting on the horizon in the west, just as it had been in the same place in 1856.

He would have his rum drink after all, he decided.

"Mother," he said, "do you think there might be anything valuable in those papers of your great-grandfather's?"

"What papers, dear? Oh—I remember. I couldn't say. I thought once of donating them to a historical society. How do you mean, valuable?"

"Well, old stamps, for one thing."

"You're free to look, Caspar dear."

Caspar was not surprised (though he supposed the rest of the world was soon to be) that he found among the faded, water-spotted diaries and papers an envelope that bore a faint brown address—it had aged nicely in the next-to-no-time it had traveled "forward" with Caspar—and that had in its upper right-hand corner a one-penny magenta stamp, quite undistinguished, issued for a brief time in 1856 by the Crown Colony of British Guiana.

The asking price of the sole known example of this stamp, a "unique" owned by a consortium of wealthy men who preferred to remain anonymous, was a million dollars. Caspar Last had not decided whether it would be more profitable for him to sell the stamp itself, or to approach the owners of the unique, who would certainly pay a large amount to have it destroyed, and thus preserve their unique's uniqueness. It did seem a shame that the only artifact man had ever succeeded in extracting from the nonexistent past should go into the fire, but Caspar didn't really care. His own bonfire—the notes and printouts, the conclusions about the nature and transversability of time and the orthogonal logic by which it was accomplished—would be only a little more painful.

The excursion was over; the only one that remained to him was the brief but, to him, all-important one of his own mortal span. He was looking forward to doing it first class.

II: An Appointment
in Khartoum

I T MIGHT BE BEGUN VERY DIFFERENTLY, THOUGH; AND IT might now be begun again, in a different time and place, like one of those romances by Stevenson, where different stories only gradually reveal themselves to be parts of a whole . . .

The paradox is acute, so acute that the only possible stance for a chronicler is to ignore it altogether, and carry on. This, the Otherhood's central resignation, required a habit of mind so contrary to ordinary cause-and-effect thinking as to be, literally, unimaginable. It would only have been in the changeless precincts of the Club they had established beyond all frames of reference, when deep in leather armchairs or seated all together around the long table whereon their names were carved, that they dared reflect on it at all.

Take, for a single but not a random instance, the example of Denys Winterset, twenty-three years old, Winchester, Oriel College, younger son of a well-to-do doctor and in 1956 ending a first year as assistant district commissioner of police in Bechuanaland.

He hadn't done strikingly well in his post. Though on the

surface he was exactly the sort of man who was chosen, or who chose himself, to serve the Empire in those years—a respectable second at Oxford, a cricketer more steady than showy, a reserved, sensible, presentable lad with sound principles and few beliefs—still there was an odd strain in him. Too imaginative, perhaps; given to fits of abstraction, even to what his commissioner called "tears, idle tears." Still, he was resourceful and hardworking; he hadn't disgraced himself, and he was now on his way north on the Cape-to-Cairo Railroad, to take a month's holiday in Cairo and England. His anticipation was marred somewhat by a sense that, after a year in the veldt, he would no longer fit into the comfortable old shoe of his childhood home; that he would feel as odd and exiled as he had in Africa. Home had become a dream, in Bechuanaland; if, at home, Bechuanaland became a dream, then he would have no place real at all to be at home in; he would be an exile for good.

The high veldt sped away as he was occupied with these thoughts, the rich farmlands of Southern Rhodesia. In the saloon car a young couple, very evidently on honeymoon, watched expectantly for the first glimpse of the eternal rainbow, visible miles off, that haloed Victoria Falls. Denys watched them and their excitement, feeling old and wise. Americans, doubtless: they had that shy, inoffensive air of all Americans abroad, that wondering quality as of children let out from a dark and oppressive school to play in the sun.

"There!" said the woman as the train took a bend. "Oh, look, how beautiful!"

Even over the train's sound they could hear the sound of the falls now, like distant cannon. The young man looked at his watch and smiled at Denys. "Right on time," he said, and Denys smiled too, amused to be complimented on his railroad's efficiency. The Bulawayo Bridge—longest and highest span on the Cape-to-Cairo line—leapt out over the gorge.

"My God, that's something," the young man said. "Cecil Rhodes built this, right?"

"No," Denys said. "He thought of it, but never lived to see it. It would have been far easier to build it a few miles up, but Rhodes pictured the train being washed in the spray of the falls as it passed. And so it was built here."

The noise of the falls was immense now, and weirdly various, a medley of cracks, thumps, and explosions playing over the constant bass roar, which was not so much like a noise at all as it was like an eternal deep-drawn breath. And as the train chugged out across the span, aimed at Cairo thousands of miles away, passing here the place so hard-sought-for a hundred years ago—the place where the Nile had its origin—the spray *did* fall on the train just as Cecil Rhodes had imagined it, flung spindrift hissing on the locomotive, drops speckling the window they looked out of and rainbowing in the white air. The young Americans were still with wonder, and Denys, too, felt a lifting of his heart.

At Khartoum, Denys bid the honeymooners farewell: they were taking the Empire Airways flying boat from here to Gibraltar, and the Atlantic dirigible home. Denys, by now feeling quite proprietary about his Empire's transportation services, assured them that both flights would also certainly be right on time, and would be as comfortable as the sleepers they were leaving, would serve the same excellent meals with the same white napery embossed with the same royal insignia. Denys himself was driven to the Grand Hotel. His Sudan Railways sleeper to Cairo left the next morning.

After a bath in a tiled tub large enough almost to swim in, Denys changed into dinner clothes (which had been carefully laid out for him on the huge bed—for whom had these cavernous rooms been built, a race of Kitcheners?) He reserved a table for one in the grill room and went down to the bar. One thing he *must* do in London, he thought, shooting his cuffs, was to visit his tailor. Bechuanaland had sweated off his college baby fat, and the tropics seemed to have turned his satin lapels faintly green.

The bar was comfortably filled, before the dinner hour, with men of several sorts and a few women, and with the low various murmur of their talk. Some of the men wore *white* dinner jackets—businessmen and tourists, Denys supposed; and a few even wore shorts with black shoes and stockings, a style Denys found inherently funny, as though a tailor had made a frightful error and cut evening clothes to the pattern of bush clothes. He ordered a whiskey.

Rarely in African kraals or in his bungalow or his whitewashed office did Denys think about his Empire: or if he did, it was in some local, even irritated way, of Imperial trivialities or Imperial red tape, the rain-rusted engines and stacks of tropic-mildewed paperwork that, collectively, Denys and his young associates called the White Man's Burden. It seemed to require a certain remove from the immediacy of Empire before he could perceive it. Only here (beneath the fans' ticking, amid the voices naming places—Kandahar, Durban, Singapore, Penang) did the larger Empire that Denys had never seen but had lived in in thought and feeling since childhood open in his mind. How odd, how far more odd really than admirable or deplorable that the small place which was his childhood, circumscribed and cozy—gray Westminster, chilly Trafalgar Square of the black umbrellas, London of the coal-smoked wallpaper and endless chimney pots—should have opened itself out so ceaselessly and for so long into huge hot places, subcontinents where rain never fell or never stopped, lush with vegetable growth or burdened with seas of sand or stone. Send forth the best ye breed: or at least large numbers of those ye breed. If one thought how odd it was— and if one thought then of what should have been natural empires, enormous spreads of restless real property like

America or Russia turning in on themselves, making themselves into what seemed (to Denys, who had never seen them) to be very small places: then it did seem to be Destiny of a kind. Not a Destiny to be proud of, particularly, nor ashamed of either, but one whose compelling inner logic could only be marveled at.

Quite suddenly, and with poignant vividness, Denys saw himself, or rather felt himself once more to be, before his nursery fire, looking into the small glow of it, with animal crackers and cocoa for tea, listening to Nana telling tales of her brother the sergeant, and the Afghan frontier, and the now-dead king he served—listening, and feeling the Empire ranged in widening circles around him: first Harley Street, outside the window, and then Buckingham Palace, where the king lived; and the country then into which the trains went, and then the cold sea, and the Possessions, and the Commonwealth, stretching ever farther outward, worldwide: but always with his small glowing fire and his comfort and wonder at the heart of it.

So, there he is: a young man with the self-possessed air of an older, in evening clothes aged prematurely in places where evening clothes had not been made to go; thinking, if it could be called thinking, of a nursery fire; and about to be spoken to by the man next down the bar. If his feelings could be summed up and spoken, they were that, however odd, there is nothing more real, more pinioned by acts great and small, more clinker-built of time and space and filled brimful of this and that, than is the real world in which his five senses and his memories had their being; and that this was deeply satisfying.

"I beg your pardon," said the man next down the bar.

"Good evening," Denys said.

"My name is Davenant," the man said. He held out a square, blunt-fingered hand, and Denys drew himself up and shook it. "You are, I believe, Denys Winterset?"

"I am," Denys said, searching the smiling face before him and wondering from where he was known to him. It was a big, square, high-fronted head, a little like Bernard Shaw's, with ice-blue eyes of that twinkle; it was crowned far back with a neat hank of white hair, and was crossed above the broad jaw with upright white mustaches.

"You don't mind the intrusion?" the man said. "I wonder if you know whether the grub here is as good as once it was. It's been some time since I last ate a meal in Khartoum."

"The last time I did so was a year ago this week," Denys said. "It was quite good."

"Excellent," said Davenant, looking at Denys as though something about the young man amused him. "In that case, if you have no other engagement, may I ask your company?"

"I have no other engagement," Denys said; in fact he had rather been looking forward to dining alone, but deference to his superiors (of whom this man Davenant was surely in some sense one) was strong in him. "Tell me, though, how you come to know my name."

"Oh, well, there it is," Davenant said. "One has dealings with the Colonial Office. One sees a face, a name is attached to it, one files it but doesn't forget—that sort of thing. Part of one's job."

A civil servant, an inspector of some kind. Denys felt the sinking one feels on running into one's tutor in a wine bar: the evening not well begun. "They may well be crowded for dinner," he said.

"I have reserved a quiet table," said the smiling man, lifting his glass to Denys.

The grub was, in fact, superior. Sir Geoffrey Davenant was an able teller of tales, and he had many to tell. He was, apparently, no such dull thing as an inspector for the Colonial Office, though just what office he did fill Denys couldn't determine. He seemed to have been "attached to" or "had dealings with" or "gone about for" half the establishments of the Empire. He embodied, it seemed to Denys, the entire strange adventure about which Denys had been thinking when Sir Geoffrey had first spoken to him.

"So," Sir Geoffrey said, filling their glasses from a bottle of South African claret—no harm in being patriotic, he'd said, for one bottle—"so, after some months of stumbling about Central Asia and making myself useful one way or another, I was to make my way back to Sadiya. I crossed the Tibetan frontier disguised as a monk—"

"A monk?"

"Yes. Having lost all my gear in Manchuria, I could do the poverty part quite well. I had a roll of rupees, the films, and a compass hidden inside my prayer wheel. Mine didn't whiz around then with the same sanctity as the other fellows', but no matter. After adventures too ordinary to describe— avalanches and so on—I managed to reach the monastery at Rangbok, on the old road up to Everest. Rather near collapse. I was recovering a bit and thinking how to proceed when there was a runner with a telegram. From my superior at Ch'eng-tu. WARN DAVENANT MASSACRE SADIYA, it said. The Old Man then was famously closemouthed. But this was particularly unhelpful, as it did not say who had massacred whom— or why." He lifted the silver cover of a dish, and found it empty.

"This must have been a good long time ago," Denys said.

"Oh, yes," Davenant said, raising his ice-blue eyes to Denys. "A good long time ago. That was an excellent curry. Nearly as good as at Veeraswamy's, in London—which is, strangely, the best in the world. Shall we have coffee?"

Over this, and brandy and cigars, Sir Geoffrey's stories modulated into reflections. Pleasant as his company was, Denys couldn't overcome a sensation that everything Sir

Geoffrey said to him was rehearsed, laid on for his entertainment, or perhaps his enlightenment, and yet with no clue in it as to why he had thus been singled out.

"It amuses me," Sir Geoffrey said, "how constant it is in human nature to think that things might have gone on differently from the way they did. In a man's own life, first of all: how he might have taken this or that very different route, except for this or that accident, this or that slight push—if he'd only known then, and so on. And then in history as well, we ruminate endlessly, if, what if, if only . . . The world seems always somehow malleable to our minds, or to our imaginations anyway."

"Strange you should say so," Denys said. "I was thinking, just before you spoke to me, about how very solid the world seems to me, how very—real. And—if you don't mind my thrusting it into your thoughts—you never did tell me how it is you come to know my name; or why it is you thought good to invite me to that excellent dinner."

"My dear boy," Davenant said, holding up his cigar as though to defend his innocence.

"I can't think it was chance."

"My dear boy," Davenant said in a different tone, "if anything is, that was not. I will explain all. You were on that train of thought. If you will have patience while it trundles by."

Denys said nothing further. He sipped his coffee, feeling a dew of sweat on his forehead.

"History," said Sir Geoffrey. "Yes. Of course the possible worlds we make don't compare to the real one we inhabit— not nearly so well furnished, or tricked out with details. And yet still somehow better. More satisfying. Perhaps the novelist is only a special case of a universal desire to reshape, to 'take this sorry scheme of things entire,' smash it into bits, and 'remold it nearer to the heart's desire'—as old Khayyám says.

The egoist is continually doing it with his own life. To dream of doing it with history is no more useful a game, I suppose, but as a game, it shows more sport. There are rules. You can be more objective, if that's an appropriate word.'' He seemed to grow pensive for a moment. He looked at the end of his cigar. It had gone out, but he didn't relight it.

"Take this Empire,'' he went on, drawing himself up somewhat to say it. "One doesn't want to be mawkish, but one has served it. Extended it a bit, made it more secure; done one's bit. You and I. Nothing more natural, then, if we have worked for its extension in the future, to imagine its extension in the past. We can put our finger on the occasional bungle, the missed chance, the wrong man in the wrong place, and so on, and we think: if I had only been there, seen to it that the news went through, got the guns there in time, forced the issue at a certain moment—well. But as long as one is dreaming, why stop? A favorite instance of mine is the American civil war. We came very close, you know, to entering that war on the Confederacy's side.''

"Did we.''

"I think we did. Suppose we had. Suppose we had at first dabbled—sent arms—ignored Northern protests—then got deeper in; suppose the North declared war on us. It seems to me a near certainty that if we had entered the war fully, the South would have won. And I think a British presence would have mitigated the slaughter. There was a point, you know, late in that war, when a new draft call in the North was met with terrible riots. In New York several Negroes were hanged, just to show how little their cause was felt.''

Denys had partly lost the thread of this story, unable to imagine himself in it. He thought of the Americans he had met on the train. "Is that so,'' he said.

"Once having divided the States into two nations, and having helped the South to win, we would have been in place, you see. The fate of the West had not yet been decided. With the North much diminished in power—well, I imagine that by now we—the Empire—would have recouped much of what we lost in 1780."

Denys contemplated this. "Rather stirring," he said mildly. "Rather cold-blooded, too. Wouldn't it have meant condoning slavery? To say nothing of the lives lost. British, I mean."

"Condoning slavery—for a time. I've no doubt the South could have been bullied out of it. Without, perhaps, the awful results that accompanied the Northerners doing it. The eternal resentment. The backlash. The near genocide of the last hundred years. And, in my vision, there would have been a net savings in red men." He smiled. "Whatever might be said against it, the British Empire does not wipe out populations wholesale, as the Americans did in their West. I often wonder if that sin isn't what makes the Americans so gloomy now, so introverted."

Denys nodded. He believed implicitly that his Empire did not wipe out populations wholesale. "Of course," he said, "there's no telling what exactly would have been the result. If we'd interfered as you say."

"No," Sir Geoffrey said. "No doubt whatever result it *did* have would have to be reshaped as well. And the results of that reshaping reshaped, too, the whole thing subtly guided all along its way toward the result desired—after all, if we can imagine how we might want to alter the past we do inherit, so we can imagine that any past might well be liable to the same imagining; that stupidities, blunders, shortsightedness, would occur in any past we might initiate. Oh, yes, it would all have to be reshaped, with each reshaping. . . ."

"The possibilities are endless," Denys said, laughing. "I'm afraid the game's beyond me. I say let the North win—since in any case we can't do the smallest thing about it."

"No," Davenant said, grown sad again, or reflective; he seemed to feel what Denys said deeply. "No, we can't. It's just—just too long ago." With great gravity he relit his cigar. Denys, at the oddness of this response, seeing Sir Geoffrey's eyes veiled, thought: *Perhaps he's mad.* He said, joining the game, "Suppose, though. Suppose Cecil Rhodes hadn't died young, as he did. . . ."

Davenant's eyes caught cold fire again, and his cigar paused in midair. "Hm?" he said with interest.

"I only meant," Denys said, "that your remark about the British not wiping out peoples wholesale was perhaps not tested. If Rhodes had lived to build his empire—hadn't he already named it Rhodesia?—I imagine he would have dealt fairly harshly with the natives."

"Very harshly," said Sir Geoffrey.

"Well," Denys said, "I suppose I mean that it's not always evil effects that we inherit from these past accidents."

"Not at all," said Sir Geoffrey. Denys looked away from his regard, which had grown, without losing a certain cool humor, intense. "Do you know, by the way, that remark of George Santayana—the American philosopher—about the British Empire, about young men like yourself? 'Never,' he said, 'never since the Athenians has the world been ruled by such sweet, just, boyish masters.' "

Denys, absurdly, felt himself flush with embarrassment.

"I don't ramble," Sir Geoffrey said. "My trains of thought carry odd goods, but all headed the same way. I want to tell you something, about that historical circumstance, the one you've touched on, whose effects we inherit. Evil or good I will leave you to decide.

"Cecil Rhodes died prematurely, as you say. But not before he had amassed a very great fortune, and laid firm claims to the ground where that fortune would grow far greater. And also not before he had made a will disposing of that fortune."

"I've heard stories," Denys said.

"The stories you have heard are true. Cecil Rhodes, at his death, left his entire fortune, and its increase, to found and continue a secret society which should, by whatever means possible, preserve and extend the British Empire. His entire fortune."

"I have never believed it," Denys said, momentarily feeling untethered, like a balloon: afloat.

"For good reason," Davenant said. "If such a society as I describe were brought into being, its very first task would be to disguise, cast doubt upon, and quite bury its origins. Don't you think that's so? In any case it's true what I say: the society was founded; is secret; continues to exist; is responsible, in some large degree at least, for the Empire we now know, in this year of grace 1956, IV Elizabeth II, the Empire on which the sun does not set."

The veranda where the two men sat was nearly deserted now; the night was loud with tropical noises that Denys had come to think of as silence, but the human noise of the town had nearly ceased.

"You can't know that," Denys said. "If you knew it, if you were privy to it, then you wouldn't say it. Not to me." He almost added: *Therefore you're not in possession of any secret, only a madman's certainty.*

"I *am* privy to it," Davenant said. "I am myself a member. The reason I reveal the secret to you—and you see, here we are, come to you and my odd knowledge of you, at last, as I promised—the reason I reveal it to you is because I wish to ask you to join it. To accept from me an offer of membership."

Denys said nothing. A dark waiter in white crept close, and was waved away by Sir Geoffrey.

"You are quite properly silent," Sir Geoffrey said. "Either I am mad, you think, in which case there is nothing to say; or what I am telling you is true, which likewise leaves you nothing to say. Quite proper. In your place I would be silent also. In your place I was. In any case I have no intention of pressing you for an answer now. I happen to know, by a roundabout sort of means that if I explained to you would certainly convince you I was mad, that you will seriously consider what I've said to you. Later. On your long ride to Cairo: there will be time to think. In London. I ask nothing from you now. Only . . ."

He reached into his waistcoat pocket. Denys watched, fascinated: would he draw out some sign of power, a royal charter, some awesome seal? No: it was a small metal plate, with a strip of brown ribbon affixed to it, like a bit of recording tape. He turned it in his hands thoughtfully. "The difficulty, you see, is that in order to alter history and bring it closer to the heart's desire, it would be necessary to stand outside it altogether. Like Archimedes, who said that if he had a lever long enough, and a place to stand, he could move the world."

He passed the metal plate to Denys, who took it reluctantly.

"A place to stand, you see," Sir Geoffrey said. "A place to stand. I would like you to keep that plate about you, and not misplace it. It's in the nature of a key, though it mayn't look it; and it will let you into a very good London club, though it mayn't look it either, where I would like you to call on me. If, even out of simple curiosity, you would like to hear more of us." He extinguished his cigar. "I am going to describe the rather complicated way in which that key is to be used—I really do apologize for the hugger-mugger, but you will come to understand—and then I am going to bid you good evening. Your train is an early one? I thought so. My own departs at midnight. I possess a veritable Bradshaw's of the

59

world's railroads in this skull. Well. No more. I will just sign this—oh, don't thank me. Dear boy: don't thank me."

When he was gone, Denys sat a long time with his cold cigar in his hand and the night around him. The amounts of wine and brandy he had been given seemed to have evaporated from him into the humid air, leaving him feeling cool, clear, and unreal. When at last he rose to go, he inserted the flimsy plate into his waistcoat pocket; and before he went to bed, to lie a long time awake, he changed it to the waistcoat pocket of the pale suit he would wear next morning.

As Sir Geoffrey suggested he would, he thought on his ride north of all that he had been told, trying to reassemble it in some more reasonable, more everyday fashion: as all day long beside the train the sempiternal Nile—camels, nomads, women washing in the barge canals, the thin line of palms screening the white desert beyond—slipped past. At evening, when at length he lowered the shade of his compartment window on the poignant blue sky pierced with stars, he thought suddenly: But how could he have known he would find me there, at the bar of the Grand, on that night of this year, at that hour of the evening, just as though we had some long-standing agreement to meet there?

If anything is chance, Davenant had said, that was not.

At the airfield at Ismailia there was a surprise: his flight home on the R101, which his father had booked months ago as a special treat for Denys, was to be that grand old airship's last scheduled flight. The oldest airship in the British fleet, commissioned in the year Denys was born, was to be—mothballed? Drydocked? Deflated? Denys wondered just what one did with a decommissioned airship larger than Westminster Cathedral.

Before dawn it was drawn from its great hangar by a crowd of white-clothed fellahin pulling at its ropes—descendants, Denys thought, of those who had pulled ropes at the

Pyramids three thousand years ago, employed now on an object almost as big but lighter than air. It isn't because it is so intensely romantic that great airships must always arrive or depart at dawn or at evening, but only that then the air is cool and most likely to be still: and yet intensely romantic it remains. Denys, standing at the broad, canted windows, watched the ground recede—magically, for there was no sound of engines, no jolt to indicate liftoff, only the waving, cheering fellahin growing smaller. The band on the tarmac played "Land of Hope and Glory." Almost invisible to watchers on the ground—because of its heat-reflective silver dome —the immense ovoid turned delicately in the wind as it arose.

"Well, it's the end of an era," a red-faced man in a checked suit said to Denys. "In ten years they'll all be gone, these big airships. The propeller chaps will have taken over; and the jet aeroplane, too, I shouldn't wonder."

"I should be sorry to see that," Denys said. "I've loved airships since I was a boy."

"Well, they're just that little bit slower," the red-faced man said sadly. "It's all hurry-up, nowadays. Faster, faster. And for what? I put it to you: for what?"

Now with further gentle pushes of its Rolls-Royce engines, the R101 altered its attitude again; passengers at the lounge windows pointed out the Suez Canal, and the ships passing; Lake Mareotis; Alexandria, like a mirage; British North Africa, as far to the left as one cared to point; and the white-fringed sea. Champagne was being called for, traditional despite the hour, and the red-faced man pressed a glass on Denys.

"The end of an era," he said again, raising his flute of champagne solemnly.

And then the cloudscape beyond the windows shifted, and all Africa had slipped into the south, or into the imaginary, for they had already begun to seem the same thing to

Denys. He turned from the windows and decided—the effort to decide it seemed not so great here aloft, amid the potted palms and the wicker, with this pale champagne—that the conversation he had had down in the flat lands far away must have been imaginary as well.

III: The Tale of the President Pro Tem

THE UNIVERSE PROCEEDS OUT OF WHAT IT HAS BEEN and into what it will be, inexorably, unstoppably, at the rate of one second per second, one year per year, forever. At right angles to its forward progress lie the past and the future. The future, that is to say, does not lie "ahead" of the present in the stream of time, but at a right angle to it: the future of any present moment can be projected as far as you like outward from it, infinitely in fact, but when the universe has proceeded further, and a new present moment has succeeded this one, the future of this one retreats with it into the what-has-been, forever outdated. It is similar but more complicated with the past.

Now within the great process or procession that the universe makes, there can be no question of "movement," either "forward" or "back." The very idea is contradictory. Any conceivable movement is into the orthogonal futures and pasts that fluoresce from the universe as it is; and from those orthogonal futures and pasts into others, and others, and still others, never returning, always moving at right angles to the stream of time. To the traveler, therefore, who does not ever return from the futures or pasts into which he has gone, it must appear that the times he inhabits grow progressively more remote from the stream of time that generated them, the stream that has since moved on and left his futures behind. Indeed, the longer he remains in the future, the farther off the traveler gets from the moment in actuality whence he started, and the less like actuality the universe he stands in seems to him to be.

It was thoughts of this sort, only inchoate as yet and with the necessary conclusions not yet drawn, that occupied the mind of the President *pro tem* of the Otherhood as he walked the vast length of an iron and glass railway station in the capital city of an aged empire. He stopped to take a cigar case from within the black Norfolk overcoat he wore, and a cigar from the case; this he lit, and with its successive blue clouds hanging lightly about his hat and head, he walked on. There were hominids at work on the glossy engines of the empire's trains that came and went from this terminus; hominids pushing with their long strong arms the carts burdened with the goods and luggage that the trains were to carry; hominids of other sorts gathered in groups or standing singly at the barricades, clutching their tickets, waiting to depart, some aided by or waited upon by other species—too few creatures, in all, to dispel the extraordinary impression of smoky empty hugeness that the cast-iron arches of the shed made.

The President *pro tem* was certain, or at any rate retained a distinct impression, that at his arrival some days before there were telephones available for citizens to use, in the streets, in public places such as this (he seemed to see an example in his mind, a wooden box whose bright veneer was loosening in the damp climate, a complex instrument within, of enameled steel and heavy celluloid); but if there ever had been, there were none now. Instead he went in at a door above which a yellow globe was alight, a winged foot etched upon it. He chose a telegraph form from a stack of them on a long scarred counter, and with the scratchy pen provided he dashed off a quick note to the Magus in whose apartments he had been staying, telling him that he had returned late from the country and would not be with him till evening.

This missive he handed in at the grille, paying what was asked in large coins; then he went out, up the brass-railed stairs, and into the afternoon, into the quiet and familiar city.

It was the familiarity that had been, from the beginning, the oddest thing. The President *pro tem* was a man who, in the long course of his work for the Otherhood, had become accustomed to stepping out of his London club into a world not quite the same as the world he had left to enter that club. He was used to finding himself in a London—or a Lahore or a Laos—stripped of well-known monuments, with public buildings and private ways unknown to him, and a newspaper (bought with an unfamiliar coin found in his pocket) full of names that should not have been there, or missing events that should have been. But here—where nothing, nothing at all, was as he had known it, no trace remaining of the history he had come from—here where no man should have been able to take steps, where even Caspar Last had thought it not possible to take steps—the President *pro tem* could not help but feel easy: had felt easy from the beginning. He walked up the cobbled streets, his furled umbrella over his shoulder, troubled by nothing but the weird grasp that this unknown dark city had on his heart.

The rain that had somewhat spoiled his day in the country had ceased but had left a pale, still mist over the city, a humid atmosphere that gave to views down avenues a stage-set quality, each receding rank of buildings fainter, more vaguely executed. Trees, too, huge and weeping, still and featureless as though painted on successive scrims. At the great gates, topped with garlanded urns, of a public park, the President *pro tem* looked in toward the piled and sounding waters of a fountain and the dim towers of poplar trees. And as he stood resting on his umbrella, lifting the last of the cigar to his lips, someone passed by him and entered the park.

For a moment the President *pro tem* stood unmoving, thinking what an attractive person (boy? girl?) that had been, and how the smile paid to him in passing seemed to indicate a knowledge of him, a knowledge that gave pleasure or at least amusement; then he dropped his cigar end and passed through the gates through which the figure had gone.

That had *not* been a hominid who had smiled at him. It was not a Magus and surely not one of the draconics either. Why he was sure he could not have said: for the same unsayable reason that he knew this city in this world, this park, these marble urns, these leaf-littered paths. He was sure that the person he had seen belonged to a different species from himself, and different also from the other species who lived in this world.

At the fountain where the paths crossed, he paused, looking this way and that, his heart beating hard and filled absurdly with a sense of loss. The child (had it been a child?) was gone, could not be seen that way, or that way—but then was there again suddenly, down at the end of a yew alley, loitering, not looking his way. Thinking at first to sneak up on her, or him, along the sheltering yews, the President *pro tem* took a sly step that way; then, ashamed, he thought better of it and set off down the path at an even pace, as one would approach a young horse or a tame deer. The one he walked toward took no notice of him, appeared lost in thought, eyes cast down.

Indescribably lovely, the President *pro tem* thought: and yet at the same time negligent and easeful and ordinary. Barefoot, or in light sandals of some kind, light pale clothing that seemed to be part of her, like a bird's dress—and a wristwatch, incongruous, yet not really incongruous at all: someone for whom incongruity was inconceivable. A reverence—almost a holy dread—came over the President *pro tem* as he came closer: as though he had stumbled into a sacred grove. Then the one he walked toward looked up at him, which caused the President *pro tem* to stop still as if a gun had casually been turned on him.

He was known, he understood, to this person. She, or he, stared unembarrassed at the President *pro tem,* with a gaze of the most intense and yet impersonal tenderness, of compassion and amusement and calm interest all mixed; and almost imperceptibly shook her head *no* and smiled again: and the President *pro tem* lowered his eyes, unable to meet that gaze. When he looked up again, the person was gone.

Hesitantly the President *pro tem* walked to the end of the avenue of yews and looked in all directions. No one. A kind of fear flew over him, felt in his breast like the beat of departing wings. He seemed to know, for the first time, what those encounters with gods had been like, when there had been gods; encounters he had puzzled out of the Greek in school.

Anyway he was alone now in the park: he was sure of that. At length he found his way out again into the twilight streets.

By evening he had crossed the city and was climbing the steps of a tall town house, searching in his pockets for the key given him. Beside the varnished door was a small plaque, which said that within were the offices of the Orient Aid Society; but this was not in fact the case. Inside was a tall foyer; a glass-paneled door let him into a hallway wainscoted in dark wood. A pile of gumboots and rubber overshoes in a corner, macs and umbrellas on an ebony tree. Smells of tea, done with, and dinner cooking: a stew, an apple tart, a roast fowl. The tulip-shaped gas lamps along the hall were lit.

He let himself into the library at the hall's end; velvet armchairs regarded the coal fire, and on a drum table a tray of tea things consorted with the books and the papers. The President *pro tem* went to the low shelves that ran beneath the windows and drew out one volume of an old encyclopedia, buckram-bound, with marbled fore-edges and illustrations in brownish photogravure.

The Races. For some reason the major headings and certain other words were in the orthography he knew, but not the closely printed text. His fingers ran down the columns, which were broken into numbered sections headed by the names of species and subspecies. *Hominidae,* with three subspecies. *Draconiidae,* with four: here were etchings of skulls. And lastly *Sylphidae,* with an uncertain number of subspecies. Sylphidae, the Sylphids. Fairies.

"Angels," said a voice behind him. The President *pro tem* turned to see the Magus whose guest he was, recently risen no doubt, in a voluminous dressing gown richly figured. His beard and hair were so long and fine they seemed to float on the currents of air in the room, like filaments of thistledown.

" 'Angels,' is that what you call them?"

"What they would have themselves called," said the Magus. "What name they call themselves, among themselves, no one knows but they."

"I think I met with one this evening."

"Yes."

There was no photogravure to accompany the subsection on Sylphidae in the encyclopedia. "I'm sure I met with one."

"They are gathering, then."

"Not . . . not because of me?"

"Because of you."

"How, though," said the President *pro tem,* feeling again within him the sense of loss, of beating wings departing, "how, how could they have known, how . . ."

The Magus turned away from him to the fire, to the armchairs and the drum table. The President *pro tem* saw that beside one chair a glass of whiskey had been placed, and an ashtray. "Come," said the Magus. "Sit. Continue your tale. It will perhaps become clear to you: perhaps not." He sat then himself, and without looking back at the President *pro tem* he said: "Shall we go on?"

The President *pro tem* knew it was idle to dispute with his host. He did stand unmoving for the space of several heartbeats. Then he took his chair, drew the cigar case from his pocket, and considered where he had left off his tale in the dark of the morning.

"Of course," he said then, "Last knew: he knew, without admitting it to himself, as a good orthogonist must never do, that the world he had returned to from his excursion was not the world he had left. The past he had passed through on his way back was not 'behind' his present at all, but at a right angle to it; the future of that past, which he had to traverse in order to get back again, was not the same road, and 'back' was not where he got. The frame house on Maple Street which, a little sunburned, he reentered on his return was twice removed in reality from the one he had left a week before; the mother he kissed likewise.

"He knew that, for it was predicated by orthogonal logic, and orthogonal logic was in fact what Last had discovered— the transversability of time was only an effect of that discovery. He knew it, and despite his glee over his triumph, he kept his eye open. Sooner or later he would come upon something, something that would betray the fact that this world was not his.

"He could not have guessed it would be me."

The Magus did not look at the President *pro tem* as he was told this story; his pale gray eyes instead wandered from object to object around the great dark library but seemed to see none of them; what, the President *pro tem* wondered, did they see? He had at first supposed the race of Magi to be blind, from this habitual appearance of theirs; he now knew quite well that they were not blind, not blind at all.

"Go on," the Magus said.

"So," said the President *pro tem,* "Last returns from his excursion. A week passes uneventfully. Then one morning he hears his mother call: he has a visitor. Last, pretending annoyance at this interruption of his work (actually he was calculating various forms of compound interest on a half million dollars) comes to the door. There on the step is a figure in tweeds and a bowler hat, leaning on a furled umbrella: me.

" 'Mr. Last,' I said. 'I think we have business.'

"You could see by his expression that he knew I should not have been there, should not have had business with him at all. He really ought to have refused to see me. A good deal of trouble might have been saved if he had. There was no way I could force him, after all. But he didn't refuse; after a goggle-eyed moment he brought me in, up a flight of stairs (Mama waiting anxiously at the bottom), and into his study.

"Geniuses are popularly supposed to live in an atmosphere of the greatest confusion and untidiness, but this wasn't true of Last. The study—it was his bedroom, too—was of a monkish neatness. There was no sign that he worked there, except for a computer terminal, and even it was hidden beneath a cozy that Mama had made for it and Caspar had not dared to spurn.

"He was trembling slightly, poor fellow, and had no idea of the social graces. He only turned to me—his eyeglasses were the kind that oddly diffract the eyes behind and make them unmeetable—and said, 'What do you want?' "

The President *pro tem* caressed the ashtray with the tip of his cigar. He had been offered no tea, and he felt the lack.

"We engaged in some preliminary fencing," he continued. "I told him what I had come to acquire. He said he didn't know what I was talking about. I said I thought he did. He laughed and said there must be some mistake. I said, no mistake, Mr. Last. At length he grew silent, and I could see even behind those absurd goggles that he had begun to try to account for me.

"Thinking out the puzzles of orthogonal logic, you see, is not entirely unlike puzzling out moves in chess: theoretically chess can be played by patiently working out the likely consequences of each move, and the consequences of those consequences, and so on; but in fact it is not so played, certainly not by master players. Masters seem to have a more immediate apprehension of possibilities, an almost visceral understanding of the, however, rigorously mathematical logic of the board and pieces, an understanding that they can act on without being able necessarily to explain. Whatever sort of mendacious and feckless fool Caspar Last was in many ways, he was a genius in one or two, and orthogonal logic was one of them.

" 'From when,' he said, 'have you come?'

" 'From not far on,' I answered. He sat then, resigned, stuck in a sort of check impossible to think one's way out of, yet not mated. 'Then,' he said, 'go back the same way you came.'

" 'I cannot,' I said, 'until you explain to me how it is done.'

" 'You know how,' he said, 'if you can come here to ask me.'

" 'Not until you have explained it to me. Now or later.'

" 'I never will,' he said.

" 'You will,' I said. 'You will have done already, before I leave. Otherwise I would not be here now asking. Let us,' I said, and took a seat myself, 'let us assume these preliminaries have been gone through, for they have been of course, and move ahead to the bargaining. My firm are prepared to make you a quite generous offer.'

"That was what convinced him that he must, finally, give up to us the processes he had discovered, which he really had firmly intended to destroy forever: the fact that I had come there to ask for them. Which meant that he had already somehow, somewhen, already yielded them up to us."

The President *pro tem* paused again, and lifted his untouched whiskey. "It was the same argument," he said, "the same incontrovertible argument, that was used to convince me once, too, to do a dreadful thing."

He drank, thoughtfully, or at least (he supposed) appearing thoughtful; more and more often as he grew older it happened that in the midst of an anecdote, a relation, even one of supreme importance, he would begin to forget what it was he was telling; the terrifically improbable events would begin to seem not only improbable but fictitious, without insides, the incidents and characters as false as in any tawdry cinema story, even his own part in them unreal: as though they happened to someone made up—certainly not to him who told them. Often enough he forgot the plot.

"You see," he said, "Last exited from a universe in which travel 'through time' was, apparently, either not possible, or possible only under conditions that would allow such travel to go undetected. That was apparent from the fact that no one, so far as Last knew, up to the time of his own single excursion, had ever detected it going on. No one from Last's own future, that is, had ever come 'back' and disrupted his present, or the past of his present: never ever. Therefore, if his excursion could take place, and he could 'return,' he would have to return to a different universe: a universe where time travel *had* taken place, a universe in which once-upon-a-time a man from 1983 had managed to insert himself into a minor colony of the British Crown one hundred and twenty-seven years earlier. What he couldn't know in advance was whether the universe he 'returned' to was one where time travel was a commonplace, an everyday occurrence, something anyway that could deprive his excursion of the value it had; or whether it was one in which one excursion only had taken place, his own. My appearance before him convinced him that it was, or was about to become, common enough: common enough to disturb his own peace and quiet, and alter in unforeseeable ways his comfortable present.

"There was only one solution, or one dash at a solution anyway. I might, myself, be a singularity in Last's new present. It was therefore possible that if he could get rid of me, I would take his process 'away' with me into whatever future I had come out of to get it, and thereupon never be able to find my way again to his present and disturb it or him. Whatever worlds I altered, they would not be his, not his anyway who struck the bargain with me: if each of them also contained a Last, who would suffer or flourish in ways unimaginable to the Last to whom I spoke, then those eidolons would have to make terms for themselves, that's all. The quantum angle obtended by my coming, and then the one obtended by my returning, divorced all those Lasts from him for all eternity: that is why, though the angle itself is virtually infinitesimal, it has always to be treated as a right angle.

"Last showed me, on his computer, after our bargain was struck and he was turning over his data and plans to me. I told him I would not probably grasp the theoretical basis of the process, however well I had or would come to manage the practical paradoxes of it, but he liked to show me. He first summoned up x-y coordinates, quite ordinary, and began by showing me how some surprising results were obtained by plotting on such coordinates an imaginary number, specifically the square root of minus one. The only way to describe what happens, he said, is that the plotted figure, one unit high, one unit wide, generates a shadow square of the same measurements 'behind' itself, in space undefined by the coordinates. It was with such tricks that he had begun; the orthogons he obtained had first started him thinking about the generation of inhabitable—if also somehow imaginary—pasts.

"Then he showed me what became of the orthogons so constructed if the upright axis were set in motion. Suppose (he said) that this vertical coordinate were in fact revolving around the axle formed by the other, horizontal coordinate. If it were so revolving, like an aeroplane propeller, we could not apprehend it, edge on as it is to us, so to speak; but what would that motion do to the plots we were making? And of course it was quite simple, given the proper instructions to the computer, to find out. And his orthogons—always remaining at right angles to the original coordinates—began to turn in the prop wash of the whole system's progress at one second per second out of the what-was and into the what-has-never-yet-been; and to generate, when one had come to see them, the paradoxes of orthogonal logic: the cyclonic storm of logic in which all travelers in that medium always stand; the one in which Last and I, I bending over his shoulder hat in hand, he with fat white fingers on his keys and eyeglasses slipping down his nose, stood even as we spoke: a storm as unfeelable as Last's rotating axis was unseeable."

The President *pro tem* tossed his extinguished cigar into the fading fire and crossed his arms upon his breast, weary; weary of the tale.

"I don't yet understand," the other said. "If he had been so adamant, why would he give up his secrets to you?"

"Well," said the President *pro tem,* "there was, also, the matter of money. It came down to that, in the end. We were able to make him a very generous offer, as I said."

"But he didn't need money. He had this stamp."

"Yes. So he did. Yes. We were able to pick up the stamp, too, from him, as part of the bargain. I think we offered him a hundred pounds. Perhaps it was more."

"I thought it was invaluable."

"Well, so did he, of course. And yet he was not really as surprised as one might have expected him to be, when he discovered it was not; when it turned out that the stamp he had gone to such trouble to acquire was in fact rather a common one. I seemed to see it in his face, the expectation of what he was likely to find, as soon as I directed him to look it up in his Scott's, if he didn't believe me. And there it was in Scott's: the one-penny magenta 1856, a nice enough stamp, a stamp many collectors covet, and many also have in their albums. He had begun breathing stertorously, staring down at the page. I'm afraid he was suffering, rather, and I didn't like to observe it.

" 'Come,' I said to him. 'You knew it was possible.' And he did, of course. 'Perhaps it was something you did,' I said. 'Perhaps you bought the last one of a batch, and the postmaster subsequently reordered, a thing he had not before intended to do. Perhaps . . .' But I could see him think it: there needed to be no such explanation. He needed to have made no error, nor to have influenced the moment's shape in any way by his presence. The very act of his coming and going was sufficient source of unpredictable, stochastic change: this world was not his, and minute changes from his were predicated. But *this* change, this of all possible changes . . .

"His hand had begun to shake, holding the volume of Scott's. I really wanted now to get through the business and be off, but it couldn't be hurried. I knew that, for I'd done it all before. In the end we acquired the stamp. And then destroyed it, of course."

The President *pro tem* remembered: a tiny, momentary fire.

"It's often been observed," he said, "that the cleverest scientists are often the most easily taken in by charlatans. There is a famous instance, famous in some worlds, of a scientist who was brought to believe firmly in ghosts and ectoplasm, because the medium and her manifestations passed all the tests the scientist could devise. The only thing he didn't think to test for was conscious fraud. I suppose it's because the phenomena of nature, or the entities of mathematics, however puzzling and elusive they may be, are not after all bent on fooling the observer; and so a motive that would be evident to the dullest of policemen does not occur to the genius."

"The stamp," said the Magus.

"The stamp, yes. I'm not exactly proud of this part of the story. We were convinced, though, that two *very* small wrongs could go a long way toward making a very great right. And Last, who understood me and the 'firm' I represented to be capable of handling—at least in a practical way—the awful paradoxes of orthogony, did not imagine us to be also skilled, if anything more skilled, at such things as burglary, uttering, fraud, and force. Of such contradictions is Empire made. It was easy enough for us to replace, while Last was off in the tropics, one volume of his Scott's stamp catalog with another printed by ourselves, almost identical to his but containing one difference. It was harder waiting to see, once he had looked up his stamp in our bogus volume, if he would then search out some other source to confirm what he found there. He did not."

The Magus rose slowly from his chair with the articulated dignity, the wasteless lion's motion, of his kind. He tugged the bell pull. He picked up the poker then, and stood with his hand upon the mantel, looking down into the ruby ash of the dying fire. "I would he had," he said.

The dark double doors of the library opened, and the servant entered noiselessly.

"Refresh the gentleman's glass," the Magus said without turning from the fire, "and draw the drapes."

The President *pro tem* thought that no matter how long he lived in this world he would never grow accustomed to the presence of draconics. The servant's dark hand lifted the decanter, poured an exact dram into the glass, and stoppered the bottle again; then his yellow eyes, irises slit like a cat's or a snake's, rose from that task toward the next, the drawing of the drapes. Unlike the eyes of the Magi, these draconic eyes seemed to see and weigh everything—though on a single scale, and from behind a veil of indifference.

Their kind, the President *pro tem* had learned, had been servants for uncounted ages, though the Magus his host had said that once they had been masters, and men and the other hominids their slaves. And they still had, the President *pro tem* observed, that studied reserve which upper servants had in the world from which the President *pro tem* had come, that reserve which says: Very well, I will do your bidding, better than you could do it for yourself; I will maintain the illusion of your superiority to me, as no other creature could.

With a taper he lit at the fire, he lit the lamps along the walls and masked them with glass globes. Then he drew the drapes.

"I'll ring for supper," the Magus said, and the servant stopped at the sound of his voice. "Have it sent in." The servant moved again, crossing the room on narrow naked feet. At the doorway he turned to them, but only to draw the double doors closed together as he left.

For a time the Magus stood regarding the doors the great lizard had closed. Then: "Outside the City," he said, "in the mountains, they have begun to combine. There are more stories every week. In the old forests whence they first emerged, they have begun to collect on appointed days, try-ing to remember—for they are not really as intelligent as they look—trying to remember what it is they have lost, and to think of gaining it again. In not too long a time we will begin to hear of massacres. Some remote place; a country house; a more than usually careless man; a deed of unfamiliar horrid-ness. And a sign left, the first sign: a writing in blood, or something less obvious. And like a spot symptomatic of a fatal disease, it will begin to spread."

The President *pro tem* drank, then said softly: "We didn't know, you know. We didn't understand that this would be the result." The drawing of the drapes, the lighting of the lamps, had made the old library even more familiar to the President *pro tem:* the dark varnished wood, the old tobacco smoke, the hour between tea and dinner; the draught that whispered at the window's edge, the bitter smell of the coal on the grate; the comfort of this velvet armchair's napless arms, of this whiskey. The President *pro tem* sat grasped by all this, almost unable to think of anything else. "We couldn't know."

"Last knew," the Magus said. "All false, all imaginary, all generated by the wishes and fears of others: all that I am, my head, my heart, my house. Not the world's doing, or time's, but yours." The opacity of his eyes, turned on the President *pro tem,* was fearful. "You have made me; you must unmake me."

"I'll do what I can," the President *pro tem* said. "All that I can."

"For centuries we have studied," the Magus said. "We have spent lifetimes—lifetimes much longer than yours—searching for the flaw in this world, the flaw whose existence we suspected but could not prove. I say 'centuries,' but those centuries have been illusory, have they not? We came, finally, to guess at you, down the defiles of time, working your changes, which we can but suffer.

"We only guessed at you: no more than men or beasts can we Magi remember, once the universe has become different, that it was ever other than it is now. But I think the Sylphids can feel it change: can know when the changes are wrought. Imagine the pain for them."

That was a command: and indeed the President *pro tem* could imagine it, and did. He looked down into his glass.

"That is why they are gathering. They know already of your appearance; they have expected you. The request is theirs to make, not mine: that you put this world out like a light."

He stabbed with the poker at the settling fire, and the coals gave up blue flames for a moment. The mage's eyes caught the light, and then went out.

"I long to die," he said.

IV: *Chronicles of the Otherhood*

O NCE PAST THE DOOR, OR WHAT MIGHT BE CON-
sidered the door, of what Sir Geoffrey Davenant
had told him was a club, Denys Winterset was
greeted by the Fellow in Economic History, a gentle, aca-
demic-looking man called Platt.

"Not many of the Fellows about, just now," he said.
"Most of them fossicking about on one bit of business or
another. I'm always here." He smiled, a vague, self-effacing
smile. "Be no good out there. But they also serve, eh?"

"Will Sir Geoffrey Davenant be here?" Denys asked him.
He followed Platt through what did seem to be a gentlemen's
club of the best kind: dark-paneled, smelling richly of leather
upholstery and tobacco.

"Davenant, oh, yes," said Platt. "Davenant will be here.
All the executive committee will get here, if they can. The
President—*pro tem.*" He turned back to look at Denys over
his half-glasses. "All our presidents are *pro tem.*" He led on.
"There'll be dinner in the executive committee's dining room.
After dinner we'll talk. You'll likely have questions." At that
Denys almost laughed. He felt made of questions, most of
them unputtable in any verbal form.

Platt stopped in the middle of the library. A lone Fellow in a corner by a green-shaded lamp was hidden by the *Times* held up before him. There was a fire burning placidly in the oak-framed fireplace; above it, a large and smoke-dimmed painting: a portrait of a chubby, placid man in a hard collar, thinning blond hair, eyes somehow vacant. Platt, seeing Denys's look, said: "Cecil Rhodes."

Beneath the portrait, carved into the mantelpiece, were words; Denys took a step closer to read them:

> *To Ruin the Great Work of Time*
> *& Cast the Kingdoms old*
> *Into another mould.*

"Marvell," Platt said. "That poem about Cromwell. Don't know who chose it. It's right, though. I look at it often, working here. Now. It's down that corridor, if you want to wash your hands. Would you care for a drink? We have some time to kill. Ah, Davenant."

"Hullo, Denys," said Sir Geoffrey, who had lowered his *Times.* "I'm glad you've come."

"I think we all are," said Platt, taking Denys's elbow in a gentle, almost tender grasp. "Glad you've come."

He had almost not come. If it had been merely an address, a telephone number he'd been given, he might well not have; but the metal card with its brown strip was like a string tied round his finger, making it impossible to forget he had been invited. Don't lose it, Davenant had said. So it lay in his waistcoat pocket; he touched it whenever he reached for matches there; he tried shifting it to other pockets, but wherever it was on his person he felt it. In the end he decided to use it, as much to get rid of its importunity as for any other reason—so he told himself. On a wet afternoon he went to the place Davenant had told him of, the Orient Aid Society, and found it as described, a sooty French-Gothic building, one of those private houses turned to public use, with a discreet brass plaque by the door indicating that within some sort of business is done, one can't imagine what; and inside the double doors, in the vestibule, three telephone boxes, looking identical, the first of which had the nearly invisible slit by the door. His heart for some reason beat slow and hard as he inserted the card within this slot—it was immediately snatched away, like a ticket on the Underground—and entered the box and closed the door behind him.

Though nothing moved, he felt as though he had stepped onto a moving footpath, or onto one of those trick floors in a fun house that slide beneath one's feet. He was going somewhere. The sensation was awful. Beginning to panic, he tried to get out, not knowing whether that might be dangerous, but the door would not open, and its glass could not be seen out of either. It had been transparent from outside but was somehow opaque from within. He shook the door handle fiercely. At that moment the nonmobile motion reversed itself sickeningly, and the door opened. Denys stepped out, not into the vestibule of the Orient Aid Society, but into the foyer of a club. A dim, old-fashioned foyer, with faded Turkey carpet on the stairs, and an aged porter to greet him; a desk, behind which pigeonholes held members' mail; a stand of umbrellas. It was reassuring, almost absurdly so, the "then I woke up" of a silly ghost story. But Denys didn't feel reassured, or exactly awake either.

"Evening, sir."

"Good evening."

"Still raining, sir? Take your things?"

"Thank you."

A member was coming toward him down the long corridor: Platt.

"Sir?"

Denys turned back to the porter. "Your key, sir," the man said, and gave him back the metal plate with the strip of brown ribbon on it.

"Like a lift," Davenant told him as they sipped whiskey in the bar. "Alarming, somewhat, I admit; but imagine using a lift for the first time, not knowing what its function was. Closed inside a box; sensation of movement; the doors open, and you are somewhere else. Might seem odd. Well, this is the same. Only you're not somewhere else: not exactly."

"Hm," Denys said.

"Don't dismiss it, Sir Geoffrey," said Platt. "It *is* mighty odd." He said to Denys: "The paradox is acute: it is. Completely contrary to the usual cause-and-effect thinking we all do, can't stop doing really, no matter how hard we try to adopt other habits of mind. Strictly speaking it is unthinkable: unimaginable. And yet there it is."

"Yes," Davenant said. "To ignore, without ever forgetting, the heart of the matter: that's the trick. I've met monks, Japanese, Tibetan, who know the techniques. They can be learned."

"We speak of the larger paradox," Platt said to Denys. "The door you came in by being only a small instance. The great instance being, of course, the Otherhood's existence at all: we here now sitting and talking of it."

But Denys was not talking of it. He had nothing to say. To be told that in entering the telephone box in the Orient Aid Society he had effectively exited from time and entered a precinct outside it, revolving between the actual and the hypothetical, not quite existent despite the solidity of its parquet floor and the truthful bite of its whiskey; to be told that in these changeless and atemporal halls there gathered a society —"not quite a brotherhood," Davenant said; "that would be mawkish, and untrue of these chaps; we call it an Otherhood" —of men and women who by some means could insert them-

selves into the stream of the past, and with their foreknowl-
edge alter it, and thus alter the future of that past, the future in
which they themselves had their original being; that in effect
the world Denys had come from, the world he knew, the year
1956, the whole course of things, the very cast and flavor of
his memories, were dependent on the Fellows of this Society,
and might change at any moment, though if they did he
would know nothing of it; and that he was being asked to join
them in their work—he heard the words, spoken to him with
a frightening casualness; he felt his mind fill with the notions,
though not able to do anything that might be called thinking
about them; and he had nothing to say.

"You can see," Sir Geoffrey said, looking not at Denys
but into his whiskey, "why I didn't explain all this to you in
Khartoum. The words don't come easily. Here, in the Club,
outside all frames of reference, it's possible to explain. To
describe, anyway. I suppose if we hadn't a place like this, we
should all go mad."

"I wonder," said Platt, "whether we haven't, despite it."
He looked at no one. "Gone mad, I mean."

For a moment no one spoke further. The barman glanced
at them, to see if their silence required anything of him. Then
Platt spoke again. "Of course there are restrictions," he said.
"The chap who discovered it was possible to change one's
place in time, an American, thought he had proved that it was
only possible to displace oneself into the past. In a sense, he
was correct. . . ."

"In a sense," Sir Geoffrey said. "Not quite correct. The
possibilities are larger than he supposed. Or rather will suppose, all this from your viewpoint is still to happen—which
widens the possibilities right there, you see, one man's future
being as it were another man's past. (You'll get used to it, dear
boy, shall we have another of these?) The past, as it happens,
is the only sphere of time we have any interest in; the only

sphere in which we can do good. So you see there are natural limits: the time at which this process was made workable is the forward limit; and the rear limit we have made the time of the founding of the Otherhood itself. By Cecil Rhodes's will, in 1893."

"Be pointless, you see, for the Fellows to go back before the Society existed," said Platt. "You can see that."

"One further restriction," said Sir Geoffrey. "A house rule, so to speak. We forbid a man to return to a time he has already visited, at least in the same part of the world. There is the danger—a moment's thought will show you I'm right—of bumping into oneself on a previous, or successive, mission. Unnerving, let me tell you. Unnerving completely. The trick is hard enough to master as it is."

Denys found voice. "Why?" he said. "And why me?"

"Why," said Sir Geoffrey, "is spelled out in our founding charter: to preserve and extend the British Empire in all parts of the world, and to strengthen it against all dangers. Next, to keep peace in the world, insofar as this is compatible with the first; our experience has been that it usually is the same thing. And lastly to keep fellowship among ourselves, this also subject to the first, though any conflict is unimaginable, I should hope, bickering aside."

"The Society was founded to be secret," Platt said. "Rhodes liked that idea—a sort of Jesuits of the Empire. In fact there was no real need for secrecy, not until—well, not until the Society became the Otherhood. This jaunting about in other people's histories would not be understood. So secrecy *is* important. Good thing on the whole that Rhodes insisted on it. And for sure he wouldn't have been displeased at the Society's scope. He wanted the world for England. And more. 'The moon, too,' he used to say. 'I often think of the moon.' "

"Few know of us even now," Sir Geoffrey said. "The Foreign Office, sometimes. The PM. Depending on the nature of H.M. Government at any moment, we explain more, or less. Never the part about time. That is for us alone to know. Though some have guessed a little, over the years. It's not even so much that we wish to act in secret—that was just Rhodes's silly fantasy—but well, it's just damned difficult to explain, don't you see?"

"And the Queen knows of us," Platt said. "Of course."

"I flew back with her, from Africa, that day," Davenant said. "After her father had died. I happened to be among the party. I told her a little then. Didn't want to intrude on her grief, but—it seemed the moment. In the air, over Africa. I explained more later. Plucky girl," he added. "Plucky." He drew his watch out. "And as for the second part of your question—why you?—I shall ask you to reserve that one, for a moment. We'll dine upstairs . . . Good heavens, look at the time."

Platt swallowed his drink hastily. "I remember Lord Cromer's words to us when I was a schoolboy at Leys," he said. " 'Love your country,' he said, 'tell the truth, and don't dawdle.' "

"Words to live by," Sir Geoffrey said, examining the bar chit doubtfully and fumbling for a pen.

The drapes were drawn in the executive dining room; the members of the executive committee were just taking their seats around a long mahogany table, scarred around its edge with what seemed to be initials and dates. The members were of all ages; some sunburned, some pale, some in evening clothes of a cut unfamiliar to Denys; among them were two Indians and a Chinaman. When they were all seated, Denys beside Platt, there were several seats empty. A tall woman with severe gray hair but eyes somehow kind took the head of the table.

"The President *pro tem,*" she said as she sat, "is not

returned, apparently, from his mission. I'll preside, if there are no objections."

"Oh, balls," said a broad-faced man with the tan of a cinema actor. "Don't give yourself airs, Huntington. Will we really need any presiding?"

"Might be a swearing-in," Huntington said mildly, pressing the bell beside her and not glancing at Denys. "In any case, best to keep up the forms. First order of business—the soup."

It was a mulligatawny, saffrony and various; it was followed by a whiting, and that by a baron of claret-colored beef. Through the clashings of silverware and crystal Denys listened to the table's talk, little enough of which he could understand: only now and then he felt—as though he were coming horribly in two—the import of the Fellows' conversation: that history was malleable, time a fiction; that nothing was necessarily as he supposed it must be. How could they bear that knowledge? How could he?

"Mr. Deng Fa-shen, there," Platt said quietly to him, "is our physicist. Orthogonal physics—as opposed to orthogonal logic—is his invention. What makes this club possible. The mechanics of it. Don't ask me to explain."

Deng Fa-shen was a fine-boned, parchment-colored man with gentle fox's eyes. Denys looked from him to the two Indians in silk. Platt said, as though reading Denys's thought: "The most disagreeable thing about old Rhodes and the Empire of his day was its racialism, of course. Absolutely unworkable, too. Nothing more impossible to sustain than a world order based on some race's supposed inherent superiority." He smiled. "It isn't the only part of Rhodes's scheme that's proved unworkable."

The informal talk began to assemble itself, with small nudges from the woman at the head of the table (who did her presiding with no pomp and few words) around a single date:

1914. Denys knew something of this date, though several of the place names spoken of (the Somme, Jutland, Gallipoli— wherever that was) meant nothing to him. Somehow, in some possible universe, 1914 had changed everything; the Fellows seemed intent on changing 1914, drawing its teeth, teeth that Denys had not known it had—or might still have once had: he felt again the sensation of coming in two, and sipped wine.

"Jutland," a Fellow was saying. "All that's needed is a bit more knowledge, a bit more jump on events. Instead of a foolish stalemate, it could be a solid victory. Then, blockade; war over in six months . . ."

"Who's our man in the Admiralty now? Carteret, isn't it? Can he—"

"Carteret," said the bronze-faced man, "was killed the last time around at Jutland." There was a silence; some of the Fellows seemed to be aware of this, and some taken by surprise. "Shows the foolishness of that kind of thinking," the man said. "Things have simply gone too far by then. That's my opinion."

Other options were put forward. That moment in what the Fellows called the Original Situation was searched for into which a small intrusion might be made, like a surgical incision, the smallest possible intrusion that would have the proper effect; then the succeeding Situation was searched, and the Situation following that, the Fellows feeling with enormous patience and care into the workings of the past and its possibilities, like a blind man weaving. At length a decision seemed to be made, without fuss or a vote taken, about this place Gallipoli, and a Turkish soldier named Mustapha Kemal, who would be apprehended and sequestered in a quick action that took or would take place there; the sun-bronzed man would see, or had seen, to it; and the talk, after a reflective moment, turned again to anecdote and speculation.

Denys listened to the stories, of desert treks and dangerous negotiations, men going into the wilderness of a past catastrophe with a precious load of penicillin or of knowledge, to save one man's life or end another's; to intercept one trivial telegram, get one bit of news through, deflect one column of troops—removing one card from the ever-building possible future of some past moment and seeing the whole of it collapse silently, unknowably, even as another was building, just as fragile but happier: he looked into the faces of the Fellows, knowing that no ruthless stratagem was beyond them, and yet knowing also that they were men of honor, with a great world's peace and benefit in their trust, though the world couldn't know it; and he felt an odd but deep thrill of privilege to be here now, wherever that was—the same sense of privilege that, as a boy, he had expected to feel (and as a man had laughed at himself for expecting to feel) upon being admitted to the ranks of those who—selflessly, though not without reward—had been chosen or had chosen themselves to serve the Empire. "The difference you make makes all the difference," his headmasterish commissioner was fond of telling Denys and his fellows; and it was a joke among them that, in their form-filling, their execution of tedious and sometimes absurd directives, they were following in the footsteps of Gordon and Milner, Warren Hastings and Raffles of Singapore. And yet—Denys perceived it with a kind of inward stillness, as though his heart flowed instead of beating—a difference *could* be made. Had been made. Went on being made, in many times and places, without fuss, without glory, with rewards for others that those others could not recognize or even imagine. He crossed his knife and fork on his plate and sat back slowly.

"This 1914 business has its tricksome aspects," Platt said to him. "Speaking in large terms, not enough can really be done within our time frames. The Situation that issues in war was firmly established well before: in the founding of the

German Empire under Prussian leadership. Bismarck. There's the man to get to, or to his financiers, most of whom were Jewish—little did they know, and all that. Even Sedan is too late, and not enough seems to be able to be made, or unmade, out of the Dreyfus affair, though that *does* fall within our provenance. No," he said. "It's all just too long ago. If only . . . Well, no use speculating, is there? Make the best of it, and shorten the war; make it less catastrophic at any rate, a short, sharp shaking-out—above all, win it quickly. We must do the best we can."

He seemed unreconciled.

Denys said: "But I don't understand. I mean, of course I wouldn't expect to understand it as you do, but . . . well, you *did* do all that. I mean we studied 1914 in school—the guns of August and all that, the 1915 Peace, the Monaco Conference. What I mean is . . ." He became conscious that the Fellows had turned their attention to him. No one else spoke. "What I mean to say is that *I* know you solved the problem, and how you solved it, in a general way; and I don't see why it remains to be solved. I don't see why you're worried." He laughed in embarrassment, looking around at the faces that looked at him.

"You're right," said Sir Geoffrey, "that you don't understand." He said it smiling, and the others were, if not smiling, patient and not censorious. "The logic of it is orthogonal. I can present you with an even more paradoxical instance. In fact I intend to present you with it; it's the reason you're here."

"The point to remember," the woman called Huntington said (as though to the whole table, but obviously for Denys's instruction), "is that here—in the Club—nothing has yet happened except the Original Situation. All is still to do: all that we have done, all still to do."

"Precisely," said Sir Geoffrey. "All still to do." He took from his waistcoat pocket an eyeglass, polished it with his napkin, and inserted it between cheek and eyebrow. "You had a question, in the bar. You asked *why me,* meaning, I suppose, why is it you should be nominated to this Fellowship, why you and not another."

"Yes," said Denys. He wanted to go on, list what he knew of his inadequacies, but kept silent.

"Let me, before answering your question, ask you this," said Sir Geoffrey. "Supposing that you were chosen by good and sufficient standards—supposing that a list had been gone over carefully, and your name was weighed; supposing that a sort of competitive examination has been passed by you— would you then accept the nomination?"

"I—" said Denys. All eyes were on him, yet they were not somehow expectant; they awaited an answer they knew. Denys seemed to know it, too. He swallowed. "I hope I should," he said.

"Very well," Sir Geoffrey said softly. "Very well." He took a breath. "Then I shall tell you that you have in fact been chosen by good and sufficient standards. Chosen, moreover, for a specific mission, a mission of the greatest importance; a mission on which the very existence of the Otherhood depends. No need to feel flattered; I'm sure you're a brave lad, and all that, but the criteria were not entirely your sterling qualities, whatever they should later turn out to be.

"To explain what I mean, I must further acquaint you with what the oldest, or rather earliest, of the Fellows call the Original Situation.

"You recall our conversation in Khartoum. I told you no lie then; it is the case, in that very pleasant world we talked in, that good year 1956, fourth of a happy reign, on that wide veranda overlooking a world at peace—it is the case, I say, in that world and in most possible worlds like it, that Cecil Rhodes died young, and left the entire immense fortune he had won in the Scramble for the founding of a secret society, a society dedicated to the extension of that Empire which had his entire loyalty. The then Government's extreme confusion over this bequest, their eventual forming of a society—not without some embarrassment and doubt—a society from which this present Otherhood descends, still working toward the same ends, though the British Empire is not now what Rhodes thought it to be, nor the world either in which it has its hegemony—well, one of the Fellows is working up or will work up that story, insofar as it can be told, and it is, as I say, a true one.

"But there is a situation in which it is not true. In that situation which we call Original—the spine of time from which all other possibilities fluoresce—Cecil Rhodes, it appears, changed his mind."

Sir Geoffrey paused to light a cigar. The port was passed him. A cloud of smoke issued from his mouth. "Changed his mind, you see," he said, dispersing the smoke with a wave. "He did not die young, he lived on. His character mellowed, perhaps, as the years fell away; his fortune certainly diminished. It may be that Africa disappointed him, finally; his scheme to take over Tanganyika and join the Cape-to-Cairo with a single All-Red railroad line had ended in failure . . ."

Denys opened his mouth to speak; he had only a week before taken that line. He shut his mouth again.

"Whatever it was," Sir Geoffrey said, "he changed his mind. His last will left his fortune—what was left of it—to his old university, a scholarship fund to allow Americans and others of good character to study in England. No secret society. No Otherhood."

There was a deep silence at the table. No one had altered his casual position, yet there was a stillness of utter attention. Someone poured for Denys, and the liquid rattle of port into his glass was loud.

"Thus the paradox," Sir Geoffrey said. "For it is only the

persuasions of the Otherhood that alter this Original Situation. The Otherhood must reach its fingers into the past, once we have learned how to do so; we must send our agents down along the defiles of time and intercept our own grandfather there, at the very moment when he is about to turn away from the work of generating us.

"And persuade him not to, you see; cause him—cause him not to turn away from that work of generation. Yes, cause him not to turn away. And thus ensure our own eventual existence."

Sir Geoffrey pushed back his chair and rose. He turned toward the sideboard, then back again to Denys. "Did I hear you say 'That's madness'?" he asked.

"No," Denys said.

"Oh," Sir Geoffrey said. "I thought you spoke. Or thought I remembered you speaking." He turned again to the sideboard, and returned again to the table with his cigar clenched in his teeth and a small box in his hands. He put this on the table. "You do follow me thus far," he said, his hands on the box and his eyes regarding Denys from under their curling brows.

"Follow you?"

"The man had to die," Sir Geoffrey said. He unlatched the box. "It was his moment. The moment you will find in any biography of him you pick up. Young, or anyway not old; at the height of his triumphs. It would have been downhill for him from there anyway."

"How," Denys asked, and something in his throat intruded on the question; it was a moment before he could complete it: "How did he die?"

"Oh, various ways," Sir Geoffrey said. "In the most useful version, he was shot to death by a young man he'd invited up to his house at Cape Town. Shot twice, in the heart, with a Webley .38-caliber revolver." He took from the box this weapon, and placed it with its handle toward Denys.

"That's madness," Denys said. His hands lay along the arms of his chair, drawing back from the gun. "You can't mean to say you went back and *shot* him, you . . ."

"Not we, dear boy," Sir Geoffrey said. "We, generally, yes; but specifically, not we. You."

"No."

"Oh, you won't be alone—not initially, at least. I can explain why it must be you and not another; I can expound the really quite dreadful paradox of it further, if you think it would help, though it seems to me best if, for now, you simply take our word for it."

Denys felt the corners of his mouth draw down, involuntarily, tightly; his lower lip wanted to tremble. It was a sign he remembered from early childhood: what had usually followed it was a fit of truculent weeping. That could not follow, here, now: and yet he dared not allow himself to speak, for fear he would be unable. For some time, then, no one spoke.

At the head of the table Huntington pushed her empty glass away.

"Mr. Winterset," she said gently. "I wonder if I might put in a word. Sit down, Davenant, will you, just for a moment, and stop looming over us. With your permission, Mr. Winterset—Denys—I should like to describe to you a little more broadly that condition of the world we call the Original Situation."

She regarded Denys with her sad eyes, then closed her fingers together before her. She began to speak, in a low voice which more than once Denys had to lean forward to catch. She told about Rhodes's last sad bad days; she told of Rhodes's chum the despicable Dr. Jameson, and his infamous raid and the provocations that led to war with the Boers; of the shame of that war, the British defeats and the British atrocities, the brutal intransigence of both sides. She told how in those same years the European powers who confronted each other in Africa were also at work stockpiling arms and building mechanized armies of a size unheard of in the history of the world, to be finally let loose upon one another in August of 1914, unprepared for what was to become of them; armies officered by men who still lived in the previous century, but armed with weapons more dreadful than they could imagine. The machine gun: no one seemed to understand that the machine gun had changed war forever, and though the junior officers and Other Ranks soon learned it, the commanders never did. At the First Battle of the Somme wave after wave of British soldiers were sent against German machine guns, to be mown down like grain. There were a quarter of a million casualties in that battle. And yet the generals went on ordering massed attacks against machine guns for the four long years of the war.

"But they knew," Denys could not help saying. "They did know. Machine guns had been used against massed native armies for years, all over the Empire. In Afghanistan. In the Sudan. Africa. They knew."

"Yes," Huntington said. "They knew. And yet, in the Original Situation, they paid no attention. They went blindly on and made their dreadful mistakes. Why? How could they be so stupid, those generals and statesmen who in the world you knew behaved so wisely and so well? For one reason only: they lacked the help and knowledge of a group of men and women who had seen all those mistakes made, who could act in secret on what they knew, and who had the ear and the confidence of one of the governments—not the least stupid of them, either, mind you. And with all our help it was still a close-run thing."

"Damned close-run," Platt put in. "Still hangs in the balance, in fact."

"Let me go on," Huntington said.

She went on: long hands folded before her, eyes now cast down, she told how at the end a million men, a whole generation, lay dead on the European battlefield, among them men whom Denys might think the modern world could not have been made without. A grotesque tyranny calling itself Socialist had been imposed on a war-weakened Russian empire. Only the intervention of a fully mobilized United States had finally broken the awful deadlock—thereby altering the further history of the world unrecognizably. She told how the vindictive settlement inflicted on a ruined Germany (so unlike the wise dispositions of the Monaco Conference, which had simply reestablished the old pre-Bismarck patchwork of German states and princedoms) had rankled in the German spirit; how a madman had arisen and, almost unbelievably, had ridden a wave of resentment and anti-Jewish hysteria to dictatorship.

"Yes," Denys said. *"That* we didn't escape, did we? I remember that, or almost remember it; it was just before I can remember anything. Anti-Jewish riots all over Germany."

"Yes," said Huntington softly.

"Yes. Terrible. These nice funny Germans, all lederhosen and cuckoo clocks, and suddenly they show a terrible dark side. Thousands of Jews, some of them very highly placed, had to leave Germany. They lost everything. Synagogues attacked, professors fired. Even Einstein, I think, had to leave Germany for a time."

Huntington let him speak. When Denys fell silent, unable to remember more and feeling the eyes of the Fellows on him, Huntington began again. But the things she began to tell of now simply could not have happened, Denys thought; no, they were part of a monstrous, foul dream, atrocities on a scale only a psychopath could conceive, and only the total resources of a strong and perverted science achieve. When Einstein came again into the tale, and the world Huntington described drifted ignorantly and inexorably into an icy and permanent stalemate that could be broken only by the end of civilization, perhaps of life itself, Denys found a loathsome surfeit rising in his throat; he covered his face, he would hear no more.

"So you see," Huntington said, "why we think it possible that the life—nearly over, in any case—of one egotistical, racialist adventurer is worth the chance to alter that situation." She raised her eyes to Denys. "I don't say you need agree. There *is* a sticky moral question, and I don't mean to brush it aside. I only say you see how we might think so."

Denys nodded slowly. He reached out and put his hand on the pistol that had been placed before him. He lifted his eyes and met those of Sir Geoffrey Davenant, which still smiled, though his mouth and his mustaches were grave.

What they were all telling him was that he could help create a better world than the original, which Huntington had described; but that was not how Denys perceived it. What Denys perceived was that reality—reality, the world he had come from, reality sun-shot and whole—was somehow under threat from a disgusting nightmare of death, ignorance, and torture, which could invade and replace it forever unless he acted. He did not think himself capable of interfering with the world to make it better; but to defend the world he knew, the world that with all its shortcomings was life and sustenance and sense and cleanly wakefulness—yes, that he could do. Would do, with all his strength.

Which is why, of course, it was he who had been chosen to do it. He saw that in Davenant's eyes.

And of course, if he refused, he could not then be

brought here to be asked. If it was now possible for him to be asked to do this by the Otherhood, then he must have already consented, and done it. That, too, was in Davenant's silence. Denys looked down. His hand was on the Webley; and beside it, carved by a penknife into the surface of the table, almost obscured by later waxings, were the neat initials *D.W.*

"I always remember what Lord Milner said," Platt spoke into his ear. *"Everyone can help."*

V: The Tears of the President Pro Tem

"I REMEMBER," THE PRESIDENT *PRO TEM* OF THE Otherhood said, "the light: a very clear, very pure, very cool light that seemed somehow potent but reserved, as though it could do terrible blinding things, and give an unbearable heat, if it chose—well, I'm not quite sure what I mean."

There was a midnight fug in the air of the library where the President *pro tem* retold his tale. The Magus to whom he told it did not look at him; his pale gray eyes moved from object to object around the room in the aimless idiot wandering that had at first caused the President *pro tem* to believe him blind.

"The mountain was called Table Mountain—a sort of high mesa. What a place that was then—I think the most beautiful in the Empire, and young then, but not raw; a peninsula simply made to put a city on, and a city being put there, beneath the mountain: and this piercing light.

"Our party put up at the Mount Nelson Hotel, perhaps a little grand for the travelers in electroplating equipment we were pretending to be, but the incognito wasn't really important, it was chiefly to explain the presence of the Last equipment among the luggage.

"A few days were spent in reconnaissance. But you see —this is continually the impossible thing to explain—in a sense those of the party who knew the outcome were only going through the motions of conferring, mapping their victim's movements, choosing a suitable moment and all that: for they knew the story; there was only one way for it to happen, if it was to happen at all. If it was *not* to happen, then no one could predict what was to happen instead; but so long as our party was there, and preparing it, it would evidently have to happen—or would have to have had to have happened."

The President *pro tem* suddenly missed his old friend Davenant, Davenant the witty and deep, who never bumbled over his tenses, never got himself stuck in a sentence such as that one; Davenant lost now with the others in the interstices of imaginary pasthood—or rather about to be lost, in the near future, if the President *pro tem* assented to what was asked of him. "It was rather jolly," he said, "like a game rather, striving to bring about a result that you were sure had already been brought about; an old ritual, if you like, to which not much importance needed to be attached, so long as it was all done correctly . . ."

"I think," said the Magus, "you need not explain these feelings that you then had."

"Sorry," said the President *pro tem*. "The house was called Groote Schuur—that was the old Dutch name, which he'd revived, for a big granary that had stood on the property; the English had called it the Grange. It was built on the lower slopes of Devil's Peak, with a view up to the mountains, and out to sea as well. He'd only recently seen the need for a house—all his life in Africa he'd more or less pigged it in rented rooms, or stayed in his club or a hotel or even a tent pitched outside town. For a long time he roomed with Dr.

Jameson, sleeping on a little truckle bed hardly big enough for his body. But now that he'd become Prime Minister, he felt it was time for something more substantial.

"It seemed to me that it would have been easier to take him out in the bush—the *bundas,* as the Matabele say. Hire a party of natives—wait till all are asleep—ambush. He often went out into the wilds with almost no protection. There was no question of honor involved—I mean, the man had to die, one way or the other, and the more explainably or accidentally the better. But I was quite wrong—I was myself still young—and had to be put right: the one time that way was tried, the assassination initiated a punitive war against the native populations that lasted for twenty years, which ended only with the virtual extermination of the Matabele and Mashona peoples. Dreadful.

"No, it had to be the house; moreover, it had to be within a very brief span of time—a time when we knew he was there, when we knew where his will was, and *which* will it was—he made eight or nine in his lifetime—and when we knew, also, what assets were in his hands. Business and ownership were fluid things in those days; his partners were quick and subtle men; his sudden death might lose us all that we were intending to acquire by it in the way of a campaign chest, so to speak.

"So it had to be the house, in this week of this year, on this night. In fact orthogonal logic dictated it. Davenant was quite calmly sure of that. After all, that was the night when it had happened: and for sure we ought not to miss it."

That was an attempt at the sort of remark Davenant might make, and the President *pro tem* smiled at the Magus, who remained unmoved. The President *pro tem* thought it impossible that beings as wise as he knew the one before him to be, no matter how grave, could altogether lack any sense of humor. For himself, he had often thought that if he did not find funny the iron laws of orthogony he would go mad; but his jokes apparently amused only himself.

"It was not a question of getting to his house, or into it; he practically kept open house the year round, and his grounds could be walked upon by anyone. The gatekeepers were only instructed to warn walkers about the animals they might come across—he had brought in dozens of species, and he allowed all but the genuinely dangerous to roam at will. Wildebeest. Zebras. Impala. And 'human beings,' as he always called them, roamed at will, too; there were always some about. At dinner he had visitors from all over Africa, and from England and Europe as well; his bedrooms were often full. I think he hated to be alone. All of which provided a fine setting, you see, for a sensational—and insoluble—murder mystery: if only the man could be got alone, and escape made good then through these crowds of hangers-on.

"Our plan depended on a known proclivity of his, or rather two proclivities. The first was a taste he had for the company of a certain sort of a young man. He liked having them around him and could become very attached to them. There was never a breath of scandal in this—well, there was talk, but only talk. His 'angels,' people called them: good-looking, resourceful if not particularly bright, good all-rounders with a rough sense of fun—practical jokes, horseplay—but completely devoted and ready for anything he might ask them to do. He had a fair crowd of these fellows up at Groote Schuur just then. Harry Curry, his private secretary. Johnny Grimmer, a trooper who was never afraid to give him orders —like a madman's keeper, some people said, scolding him and brushing dust from his shoulders; he never objected. Bob Coryndon, another trooper. They'd all just taken on a butler for themselves, a sergeant in the Inniskillings: good-looking chap, twenty-three years old. Oddly, they had all been just that age when he'd taken an interest in them: twenty-three.

Whether that was chance or his conscious choice we didn't know.

"The other proclivity was his quickness in decision making. And this often involved the young men. The first expedition into Matabeleland had been headed up by a chap he'd met at his club one morning at breakfast just as the column was preparing for departure. Took to the chap instantly: liked his looks, liked his address. Gave him the job on the spot.

"That had worked out very well, of course—his choices often did. The pioneer column had penetrated into the heart of the *bundas,* the flag was flying over a settlement they called Fort Salisbury, and the whole of Matabeleland was in the process of being added to the Empire. Up at Groote Schuur they were kicking around possible names for the new country: Rhodia, perhaps, or Rhodesland, even Cecilia. It was that night that they settled on Rhodesia."

The President *pro tem* felt a moment's shame. There had been, when it came down to it, no doubt in his mind that what they had done had been the right thing to do: and in any case it had all happened a long time ago, more than a century ago in fact. It was not what was done, or that it had been done, only the moment of its doing, that was hard to relate: it was the picture in his mind, of an old man (though he was only forty-eight, he looked far older) sitting in the lamplight reading *The Boy's Own Paper,* as absorbed and as innocent in his absorption as a boy himself; and the vulnerable shine on his balding crown; and the tender and indifferent night: it was all that which raised a lump in the throat of the President *pro tem* and caused him to pause, and roll the tip of his cigar in the ashtray, and clear his throat before continuing.

"And so," he said, "we baited our hook. Rhodes's British South Africa Company was expanding, in the wake of the Fort Salisbury success. He was on the lookout for young men of the right sort. We presented him with one: good-looking lad, public school, cricketer; just twenty-three years old. He was the bait. The mole. The Judas."

And the bait had been taken, of course. The arrangement's having been keyed so nicely to the man's nature, a nature able to be studied from the vantage point of several decades on, it could hardly have failed. That the trick seemed so fragile, even foolish, something itself out of *The Boy's Own Paper* or a story by Henley, only increased the likelihood of its striking just the right note here: the colored fanatic, Rhodes leaving his hotel after luncheon to return to Parliament, the thug stepping out of the black noon shadows with a knife just as Rhodes mounts his carriage steps—then the young man, handily by with a stout walking stick (a gift of his father upon his departure for Africa)—the knife deflected, the would-be assassin slinking off, the great man's gratitude. You must have some reward. Not a bit, sir, anyone would have done the same; just lucky I was nearby. Come to dinner at any rate— my house on the hill—anyone can direct you. Allow me to introduce myself; my name is . . .

No need, sir, everyone knows Cecil Rhodes.

And your name is . . .

The clean hand put frankly forward, the tanned, open, boyish face smiling. My name is Denys Winterset.

"So then you see," the President *pro tem* said, "the road was open. The road up to Groote Schuur. The road that branches, in effect, to lead here: to us here now speaking of it."

"And how many times since then," the Magus said, "has the world branched? How many times has it been bent double, and broken? A thousand times, ten thousand? Each time growing smaller, having to be packed into lesser space, curling into itself like a snail's shell; growing ever weaker as the changes multiply, and more liable to failure of its fabric: how many times?"

The President *pro tem* answered nothing.

"You understand, then," the Magus said to him, "what you will be asked: to find the crossroads that leads this way and to turn the world from it."

"Yes."

"And how will you reply?"

The President *pro tem* had no better answer for this question, and he gave none. He had begun to feel at once heavy as lead and disembodied. He arose from his armchair, with some effort, and crossed the worn Turkey carpet to the tall window.

"You must leave my house now," the Magus said, rising from his chair. "There is much for me to do this night, if this world is to pass out of existence."

"Where shall I go?"

"They will find you. I think in not too long a time." Without looking back he left the room.

The President *pro tem* pushed aside the heavy drape the draconic had drawn. *Where shall I go?* He looked out the window into the square outside, deserted at this late and rainy hour. It was an irregular square, the intersection of three streets, filled with rain-wet cobbles as though with shiny eggs. It was old; it had been the view out these windows for two centuries at the least; there was nothing about it to suggest that it had not been the intersection of three streets for a good many more centuries than that.

And yet it had not been there at all only a few decades earlier, when the President *pro tem* had last walked the city outside the Orient Aid Society. Then the city had been London; it was no more. These three streets, these cobbles, had not been there in 1983; nor in 1893 either. Yet there they were, somewhere early in the twenty-first century; there they had been, too, for time out of mind, familiar no doubt to any dweller in this part of town, familiar for that matter to the

President *pro tem* who looked out at them. In each of two lamp-lit cafés on two corners of the square, a man in a soft cap held a glass and looked out into the night, unsurprised, at home.

Someone had broken the rules: there simply was no other explanation.

There had been, of course, no way for anyone, not Deng Fa-shen, not Davenant, not the President *pro tem* himself, to guess what the President *pro tem* might come upon on this, the first expedition the Otherhood was making into the future: not only did the future not exist (Deng Fa-shen was quite clear about that), but, as Davenant reminded him, the Otherhood itself, supposing the continued existence of the Otherhood, would no doubt go busily on changing things in the past far and near—shifting the ground therefore of the future the President *pro tem* was headed for. Deng Fa-shen was satisfied that that future, the ultimate future, sum of all intermediate revisions, was the only one that could be plumbed, if any could; and that was the only one the Otherhood would want to glimpse: to learn how they would do, or would come to have done; to find out, as George V whispered on his death-bed, "How is the Empire."

("Only that isn't what he said," Davenant was fond of telling. "That's what he was, understandably, reported to have said, and what the Queen and the nurses convinced themselves they heard. But he was a bit dazed there at the end, poor good old man. What he said was not 'How is the Empire,' but 'What's at the Empire,' a popular cinema. I happened," he always added gravely, "to have been with him.")

The first question had been how far "forward" the Otherhood should press; those members who thought the whole scheme insane, as Platt did, voted for next Wednesday, and bring back the Derby winners please. Deng Fa-shen was not certain the thrust could be entirely calculated: the imaginary futures of imaginary pasts were not, he thought, likely to be under the control of even the most penetrating orthogonal engineering. Sometime in the first decades of the next century was at length agreed upon, a time just beyond the voyager's own mortal span—for the house rule seemed, no one could say quite why, to apply in both directions—and for as brief a stay as was consistent with learning what was up.

The second question—who was to be the voyager—the President *pro tem* had answered by fiat, assuming an executive privilege he just at that moment claimed to exist, and cutting off further debate. (Why exactly did he insist? I'm not certain why, except that it was not out of a sense of adventure, or of fun or curiosity: whatever of those qualities he may once have had had been much worn away in his rise to the Presidency *pro tem* of the Otherhood. A sense of duty may have been part of it. It may have been to forestall the others, out of a funny sort of premonition. Duty, and premonition: of what, though? Of what?)

"It'll be quite different from any of our imaginings, you know," Davenant said, who for some reason had not vigorously contested the President's decision. "The future of all possible pasts. I envy you, I do. I should rather like to see it for myself."

Quite different from any of our imaginings: very well. The President *pro tem* had braced himself for strangeness. What he had not expected was familiarity. Familiarity—cozy as an old shoe—was certainly different from his imaginings.

And yet what was it he was familiar with? He had stepped out of his club in London and found himself to be, not in the empty corridors of the Orient Aid Society that he knew well, but in private quarters of some kind that he had never seen before. It reminded him, piercingly, of a place he did know, but what place he could not have said: some don's rich but musty rooms, some wealthy and learned bachelor's digs. How had it come to be?

And how had it come to be lit by gas?

One of the pleasant side effects (most of the members thought it pleasant) of the Otherhood's endless efforts in the world had been a general retardation in the rate of material progress: so much of that progress had been, on the one hand, the product of the disastrous wars that it was the Otherhood's chief study to prevent, and on the other hand, American. The British Empire moved more slowly, a great beast without predators, and naturally conservative; it clung to proven techniques and could impose them on the rest of the world by its weight. The telephone, the motor car, the flying boat, the wireless, all were slow to take root in the Empire that the Otherhood shaped. And yet surely, the President *pro tem* thought, electricity was in general use in London in 1893, before which date no member could alter the course of things. And gas lamps lit this place.

Pondering this, the President *pro tem* had entered the somber and apparently little-used dining room and seen the draconic standing in the little butler's pantry: silent as a statue (asleep, the President *pro tem* would later deduce, with lidless eyes only seeming to be open); a polishing-cloth in his claw, and the silver before him; his heavy jaws partly open, and his weight balanced on the thick stub of tail. He wore a baize apron and black sleeve garters to protect his clothes.

Quite different from our imaginings: and yet no conceivable amount of tinkering with the twentieth century, just beyond which the President *pro tem* theoretically stood, could have brought forth this butler, in wing collar and green apron, the soft gaslight ashine on his bald brown head.

So someone had broken the rules. Someone had dared to regress beyond 1893 and meddle in the farther past. That was not, in itself, impossible; Caspar Last had done it on his first and only excursion. It had only been thought impossible for the Otherhood to do it, because it would have taken them "back" before the Otherhood's putative existence, and therefore before the Otherhood could have wrested the techniques of such travel from Last's jealous grip, a power they acquired by already having it—that was what the President *pro tem* had firmly believed.

But it was not, apparently, so. Somewhen in that stretch of years that fell between his entrance into the telephone box of the Club and his exit from it into this familiar and impossible world, someone—many someones, or someone many times—had gone "back" far before Rhodes's death: had gone back far enough to initiate this house, this city, these races who were not men.

A million years? It couldn't have been less. It didn't seem possible it could be less.

And who, then? Deng Fa-shen, the delicate, brilliant Chinaman, who had thoughts and purposes he kept to himself; the only one of them who might have been able to overcome the theoretical limits? Or Platt, who was never satisfied with what was possible within what he called "the damned parameters"?

Or Davenant. Davenant, who was forever quoting Khayyám: *Ah, Love, couldst thou and I with Him conspire To take this sorry scheme of things entire; Would we not smash it into pieces, then Remold it nearer to the heart's desire . . .*

"There is," said the Magus behind him, "one other you have not thought of."

The President *pro tem* let fall the drape and turned from the window. The Magus stood in the doorway, a great ledger in his arms. His eyes did not meet the President *pro tem's*, and yet seemed to regard him anyway, like the blind eyes of a statue.

One other . . . Yes, the President *pro tem* saw, there *was* one other who might have done this. One other, not so good at the work perhaps as others, as Davenant for example, but who nonetheless would have been, or would come to have been, in a position to take such steps. The President *pro tem* would not have credited himself with the skill, or the nerve, or the dreadnought power. But how else to account for the familiarity, the bottomless *suitability* to him of this world he had never before seen?

"Between the time of your people's decision to plumb our world," said the Magus, "and the time of your standing here within it, you must yourself have brought it into being. I see no likelier explanation."

The President *pro tem* stood still with wonder at the efforts he was apparently to prove capable of making. A million years at least: a million years. How had he known where to begin? Where had he found, would he find, the time?

"Shall I ring," the Magus said, "or will you let yourself out?"

Deng Fa-shen had always said it, and anyone who traveled in them knew it to be so: the imaginary futures and imaginary pasts of orthogony are imaginary only in the sense that imaginary numbers (which they very much resemble) are imaginary. To a man walking within one, it alone is real, no matter how strange; it is all the others, standing at angles to it, which exist only in imagination. Nightlong the President *pro tem* walked the city, with a measured and unhurried step, but with a constant tremor winding round his rib cage, waiting for what would become of him, and observing the world he had made.

Of course it could not continue to exist. It should not ever have come into existence in the first place; his own sin (if it had been his) had summoned it out of nonbeing, and his repentance must expunge it. The Magus who had taken his confession (which the President *pro tem* had been unable to withhold from him) had drawn that conclusion: it must be put out, like a light. And yet how deeply the President *pro tem* wanted it to last forever; how deeply he believed it *ought* to last forever.

The numinous and inhuman angels, about whom nothing could be said, beings with no ascertainable business among the lesser races and yet beings without whom, the President *pro tem* was sure, this world could not go on functioning. They lived (endless?) lives unimaginable to men, and perhaps to Magi, too, who yet sought continually for knowledge of them: Magi, highest of the hominids, gentle and wise yet inflexible of purpose, living in simplicity and solitude (Were there females? Where? Doing what?) and yet from their shabby studies influencing, perhaps directing, the lives of mere men. The men, such as himself, clever and busy, with their inventions and their politics and their affairs. The lesser hominids, strong, sweet-natured, comic, like placid trolls. The draconics.

It was not simply a world inhabited by intelligent races of different kinds: it was a harder thing to grasp than that. The lives of the races constituted different universes of meaning, different constructions of reality; it was as though four or five different novels, novels of different kinds by different and differently limited writers, were to become interpenetrated and conflated: inside a gigantic Russian thing a stark and violent *policier,* and inside that something Dickensian, full of plot, humors, and eccentricity. Such an interlacing of mutually exclusive universes might be comical, like a sketch in *Punch;* it might be tragic, too. And it might be neither: it might simply be what is, the given against which all airy imaginings must finally be measured: reality.

Near dawn the President *pro tem* stood leaning on a parapet of worked stone that overlooked a streetcar round-about. A car had just ended its journey there, and the conductor and the motorman descended, squat hominids in greatcoats and peaked caps. With their long strong arms they began to swing the car around for its return journey. The President *pro tem* gazed down at this commonplace sight; his nose seemed to know the smell of that car's interior, his bottom to know the feel of its polished seats. But he knew also that yesterday there had not been streetcars in this city. Today they had been here for decades.

No, it was no good, the President *pro tem* knew: the fabric of this world he had made—if it had been he—was fatally weakened with irreality. It was a botched job: as though he were that god of the Gnostics who made the material world, a minor god unversed in putting time together with space. He had not worked well. And how could he have supposed it would be otherwise? What had got into him, that he had dared?

"No," said the angel who stood beside him. "You should not think that it was you."

"If not me," said the President *pro tem,* "then who?"

"Come," said the angel. She (I shall say "she") slipped a small cool hand within his hand. "Let's go over the tracks, and into the trees beyond that gate."

A hard and painful stone had formed in the throat of the President *pro tem.* The angel beside him led him like a daughter, like the daughter of old blind Oedipus. Within the precincts of the park—which apparently had its entrance or its entrances where the angels needed them to be—he was led down an avenue of yew and dim towers of poplar toward the piled and sounding waters of a fountain. They sat together on the fountain's marble lip.

"The Magus told me," the President *pro tem* began,

"that you can feel the alterations that we make, back then. Is that true?"

"It's like the snap of a whip infinitely long," the angel said. "The whole length of time snapped and laid out differently: not only the length of time backward to the time of the change, but the length of the future forward. We felt ourselves come into being, oldest of the Old Races (though the last your changes brought into existence); we saw in that moment the aeons of our past, and we guessed our future, too."

The President *pro tem* took out his pocket-handkerchief and pressed it to his face. He must weep, yet no tears came.

"We love this world—this only world—just as you do," she said. "We love it, and we cannot bear to feel it sicken and fail. Better that it not have been than that it die."

"I shall do all I can," said the President *pro tem.* "I shall find who has done this—I suppose I know who it was, if it wasn't me—and dissuade him. Teach him, teach him what I've learned, make him see . . ."

"You don't yet understand," the angel said with careful kindness but at the same time glancing at her wristwatch. "There is no one to tell. There is no one who went beyond the rules."

"There must have been," said the President *pro tem.* "You, your time, it just isn't that far along from ours, from mine! To make this world, this city, these races . . ."

"Not far along in time," said the angel, "but many times removed. You know it to be so: whenever you, your Otherhood, set out across the timelines, your passage generated random variation in the worlds you arrived in. Perhaps you didn't understand how those variations accumulate, here at the sum end of your journeyings."

"But the changes were so minute!" said the President *pro tem.* "Deng Fa-shen explained it. A molecule here and there, no more; the position of a distant star; some trivial thing, the name of a flower or a village. Too few, too small even to notice."

"They increase exponentially with every alteration—and your Otherhood has been busy since you last presided over them. Through the days random changes accumulate, tiny errors silting up like the blown sand that fills the streets of a desert city, that buries it at last."

"But why these changes?" asked the President *pro tem* desperately. "It can't have been chance that a world like this was the sum of those histories, it can't be. A world like *this* . . ."

"Chance, perhaps. Or it may be that as time grows softer the world grows more malleable by wishes. There is no reason to believe this, yet that is what we believe. You—all of you —could not have known that you were bringing this world into being; and yet this is the world you wanted."

She reached out to let the tossed foam of the fountain fall into her hand. The President *pro tem* thought of the bridge over the Zambezi, far away; the tossed foam of the Falls. It was true: this is what they had striven for: a world of perfect hierarchies, of no change forever. God, how they must have longed for it! The loneliness of continual change—no outback, no *bundas* so lonely. He had heard how men can be unsettled for days, for weeks, who have lived through earthquakes and felt the earth to be uncertain: what of his Fellows, who had felt time and space picked apart, never to be rewoven that way again, and not once but a hundred times? What of himself?

"I shall tell you what I see at the end of all your wishings," said the angel softly. "At the far end of the last changed world, after there is nothing left that can change. There is then only a forest, growing in the sea. I say 'forest' and I say 'sea,' though whether they are of the kind I know, or some other sort of thing, I cannot say. The sea is still and the forest is thick;

it grows upward from the black bottom, and its topmost branches reach into the sunlight, which penetrates a little into the warm upper waters. That's all. There is nothing else anywhere forever. Your wishes have come true: the Empire is quiet. There is not, nor will there be, change anymore; never will one thing be confused again with another, higher for lower, better for lesser, master for servant. Perpetual Peace."

The President *pro tem* was weeping now, painful sobs drawn up from an interior he had long kept shut and bolted. Tears ran down his cheeks, into the corners of his mouth, under his hard collar. He knew what he must do, but not how to do it.

"The Otherhood cannot be dissuaded from this," the angel said, putting a hand on the wrist of the President *pro tem*. "For all of it, including our sitting here now, all of it—and the forest in the sea—is implicit in the very creation of the Otherhood itself."

"But then . . ."

"Then the Otherhood must be uncreated."

"I can't do that."

"You must."

"No, no, I can't." He had withdrawn from her pellucid gaze, horrified. "I mean it isn't because . . . If it must be done, it must be. But not by me."

"Why?"

"It would be against the rules given me. I don't know what the result would be. I can't imagine. I don't *want* to imagine."

"Rules?"

"The Otherhood came into being," said the President *pro tem*, "when a British adventurer, Cecil Rhodes, was shot and killed by a young man called Denys Winterset."

"Then you must return and stop that killing."

"But you don't see!" said the President *pro tem* in great

distress. "The rules given the Otherhood forbid a Fellow from returning to a time and place that he formerly altered by his presence . . ."

"And . . ."

"And I am myself that same Denys Winterset."

The angel regarded the President *pro tem*—the Honorable Denys Winterset, fourteenth President *pro tem* of the Otherhood—and her translucent face registered a sweet surprise, as though the learning of something she had not known gave her pleasure. She laughed, and her laughter was not different from the plashing of the fountain by which they sat. She laughed and laughed, as the old man in his black coat and hat sat silent beside her, bewildered and afraid.

VI: The Boy David of
Hyde Park Corner

THERE ARE DAYS WHEN I SEEM GENUINELY TO RE-
member, and days when I do not remember at all:
days when I remember only that sometimes I remember. There are days on which I think I recognize another
like myself: someone walking smartly along the Strand or
Bond Street, holding the *Times* under one arm and walking a
furled umbrella with the other—a sort of military bearing,
mustaches white (older than when I seem to have known him,
but then so am I, of course), and cheeks permanently tanned
by some faraway sun. I do not catch his eye, nor he mine,
though I am tempted to stop him, to ask him . . . Later on I
wonder—if I can remember to wonder—whether he, too, is
making a chronicle, in his evenings, writing up the story: a
story that can be told in any direction, starting from anywhere,
leading on to a forest in the sea.

I won't look any longer into this chronicle I've compiled.
I shall only complete it.

My name is Denys Winterset. I was born in London in
1933; I was the only son of a Harley Street physician, and my
earliest memory is of coming upon my father in tears in his
surgery: he had just heard the news that the R101 dirigible
had crashed on its maiden flight, killing all those aboard.

NOVELTY

We lived then above my father's offices, in a little building whose nursery I remember distinctly, though I was taken to the country with the other children of London when I was only six, and that building was knocked down by a bomb in 1940. A falling wall killed my mother; my father was on ambulance duty in the East End and was spared.

He didn't know quite what to do with me, nor I with myself; I have been torn all my life between the drive to discover what others whom I love and admire expect of me, and my discovery that then I don't want to do it, really. After coming down from the University I decided, out of a certain perversity which my father could not sympathize with, to join the Colonial Service. He could not fathom why I would want to fasten myself to an enterprise that everyone save a few antediluvian colonels and letter writers to the *Times* could see was a dead animal. And I couldn't explain. Psychoanalysis later suggested that it was quite simply because no one wanted me to do it. The explanation has since come to seem insufficient to me.

That was a strange late blooming of Empire in the decade after the war, when the Colonial Office took on factitious new life, and thousands of us went out to the Colonies. The Service became larger than it had been in years, swollen with ex-officers too accustomed to military life to do anything else, and with the innocent and the confused, like myself. I ended up a junior member of a transition team in a Central African country I shall not name, helping see to it that as much was given to the new native government as they could be persuaded to accept, in the way of a parliament, a well-disciplined army, a foreign service, a judiciary.

It was not after all very much. Those institutions that the British are sure no civilized nation can do without were, in the minds of many Africans who spoke freely to me, very like those exquisite japanned toffee-boxes from Fortnum & Mason that you used often to come across in native kraals, because the chieftains and shamans loved them so, to keep their juju in. Almost as soon as I arrived, it became evident that the commander in chief of the armed forces was impatient with the pace of things, and felt the need of no special transition to African, i.e., his own, control of the state. The most our Commission were likely to accomplish was to get the British population out without a bloodbath.

Even that would not be easy. We—we young men— were saddled with the duty of explaining to aged planters that there was no one left to defend their estates against confiscation, and that under the new constitution they hadn't a leg to stand on, and that despite how dearly their overseers and house people loved them, they ought to begin seeing what they could pack into a few small trunks. On the other hand, we were to calm the fears of merchants and diamond factors, and tell them that if they all simply dashed for it, they could easily precipitate a closing of the frontiers, with incalculable results.

There came a night when, more than usually certain that not a single Brit under my care would leave the country alive, nor deserved to either, I stood at the bar of the Planters' (just renamed the Republic) Club, drinking gin and Italian (tonic hadn't been reordered in weeks) and listening to the clacking of the fans. A fellow I knew slightly as a regular here saluted me; I nodded and returned to my thoughts. A moment later I found him next to me.

"I wonder," he said, "if I might have your ear for a moment."

The expression, in his mouth, was richly comic, or perhaps it was my exhaustion. He waited for my laughter to subside before speaking. He was called Rossie, and he'd spent a good many years in Africa, doing whatever came to hand. He was one of those Englishmen whom the sun turns not brown but only gray and greasy; his eyes were always watery, the cups of his lids red and painful to look at.

"I am," he said at last, "doing a favor for a chap who would like your help."

"I'll do what I can," I said.

"This is a chap," he said, "who has been too long in this country, and would like to leave it."

"There are many in his situation."

"Not quite."

"What is his name?" I said, taking out a memorandum book. "I'll pass it on to the Commission."

"Just the point," Rossie said. He drew closer to me. At the other end of the bar loud laughter arose from a group consisting of a newly commissioned field marshal—an immense, glossy, nearly blue-black man—and his two colonels, both British, both small and lean. They laughed when the field marshal laughed, though their laugh was not so loud, nor their teeth so large and white.

"He'll want to tell you his name himself," Rossie said. "I've only brought the message. He wants to see you, to talk to you. I said I'd tell you. That's all."

"To tell us . . ."

"Not you, all of you. *You:* you."

I drank. The warm, scented liquor was thick in my throat. "Me?"

"What he asked me to ask you," Rossie said, growing impatient, "was would you come out to his place, and see him. It isn't far. He wanted you, no one else. He said I was to insist. He said you were to come alone. He'll send a boy of his. He said tell no one."

There were many reasons why a man might want to do business with the Commission privately. I could think of none why it should be done with me alone. I agreed, with a shrug. Rossie seemed immediately to put the matter out of his mind, mopped his red face, and ordered drinks for both us. By the time they were brought we were already discussing the Imperial groundnut scheme, which was to have kept this young republic self-sufficient, but which, it was now evident, would do no such thing.

I too put what had been asked of me out of my mind, with enough success that when on a windless and baking afternoon a native boy shook me awake from a nap, I could not imagine why.

"Who are you? What are you doing in my bungalow?"

He only stared down at me, as though it were he who could not think why I should be there before him. Questions in his own language got no response either. At length he backed out the door, clearly wanting me to follow; and so I did, with the dread one feels on remembering an unpleasant task one has contrived to neglect. I found him outside, standing beside my Land-Rover, ready to get aboard.

"All right," I said. "Very well." I got into the driver's seat. "Point the way."

It was a small spread of tobacco and a few dusty cattle an hour's drive from town, a low bungalow looking beaten in the ocher heat. He gave no greeting as I alighted from the Land-Rover but stood in the shadows of the porch unmoving: as though he had stood so a long time. He went back into the house as I approached, and when I went in, he was standing against the netting of the window, the light behind him. That seemed a conscious choice. He was smiling, I could tell: a strange and eager smile.

"I've waited a long time for you," he said. "I don't mind saying."

"I came as quickly as I could," I said.

"There was no way for me to know, you see," he said, "whether you'd come at all."

"Your boy was quite insistent," I said. "And Mr. Rossie—"

"I meant: to Africa." His voice was light, soft and dry. "There being so much less reason for it, now. I've wondered often. In fact I don't think a day has passed this year when I haven't wondered." Keeping his back to the sunward windows, he moved to sit on the edge of a creaking wicker sofa. "You'll want a drink," he said.

"No." The place was filled with the detritus of an African bachelor farmer's digs: empty paraffin tins, bottles, tools, hanks of rope and motor parts. He put a hand behind him without looking and put it on the bottle he was no doubt accustomed to find there. "I tried to think reasonably about it," he said, pouring a drink. "As time went on, and things began to sour here, I came to be more and more certain that no lad with any pluck would throw himself away down here. And yet I couldn't know. Whether there might not be some impulse, I don't know, traveling to you from—elsewhere. . . . I even thought of writing to you. Though whether to convince you to come or to dissuade you I'd no idea."

I sat, too. A cool sweat had gathered on my neck and the backs of my hands.

"Then," he said, "when I heard you'd come—well, I was afraid, frankly. I didn't know what to think." He dusted a fly from the rim of his glass, which he had not tasted. "You see," he said, "this was against the rules given me. That I— that I and—that you and I should meet."

Perhaps he's mad, I thought, and even as I thought it I felt intensely the experience called *déjà vu,* an experience I have always hated, hated like the nightmare. I steeled myself to respond coolly and took out my memorandum book and pencil. "I'm afraid you've rather lost me," I said—briskly I hoped. "Perhaps we'd better start with your name."

"Oh," he said, smiling again his mirthless smile, "not the hardest question first, please."

Without having, so far as I knew, the slightest reason for it, I began to feel intensely sorry for this odd dried jerky of a man, whose eyes alone seemed quick and shy. "All right," I said, "nationality, then. You are a British subject."

"Well, yes."

"Proof?" He answered nothing. "Passport?" No. "Army card? Birth certificate? Papers of any kind?" No. "Any connections in Britain? Relatives? Someone who could vouch for you, take you in?"

"No," he said. "None who could. None but you. It will have to be you."

"Now hold hard," I said.

"I don't know why I must," he said, rising suddenly and turning away to the window. "But I must. I must go back. I imagine dying here, being buried here, and my whole soul retreats in horror. I must go back. Even though I fear that, too."

He turned from the window, and in the sharp side light of the late afternoon his face was clearly the face of someone I knew. "Tell me," he said. "Mother and father. Your mother and father. They're alive?"

"No," I said. "Both dead."

"Very well," he said, "very well"; but it did not seem to be very well with him. "I'll tell you my story, then."

"I think you'd best do that."

"It's a long one."

"No matter." I had begun to feel myself transported, like a Sinbad, into somewhere that it were best I listen, and keep my counsel: and yet the first words of this specter's tale made that impossible.

"My name," he said, "is Denys Winterset."

I have come to believe, having had many years in which

125

to think about it, that it must be as he said, that an impulse from somewhere else (he meant: some previous present, some earlier version of these circumstances) must press upon such a life as mine. That I chose the Colonial Service, that I came to Africa—and not just to Africa, but to that country: well, *if anything is chance, that was not*—as I understand Sir Geoffrey Davenant to have once said.

In that long afternoon, there where I perhaps could not have helped arriving eventually, I sat and perspired, listening —though it was for a long time very nearly impossible to hear what was said to me: an appointment in Khartoum some months from now, and some decades past; a club, outside all frames of reference; the Last equipment. It was quite like listening to the unfollowable logic of a madman, as meaningless as the roar of the insects outside. I only began to hear when this aged man, older than my grandfather, told me of something that he—that I—that he and I—had once done in boyhood, something secret, trivial really and yet so shameful that even now I will not write it down; something that only Denys Winterset could know.

"There now," he said, eyes cast down. "There now, you must believe me. You *will* listen. The world has not been as you thought it to be, any more than it was as I thought it to be, when I was as you are now. I shall tell you why: and we will hope that mine is the last story that need be told."

And so it was that I heard how he had gone up the road to Groote Schuur, that evening in 1893 (a young man then of course, only twenty-three) with the Webley revolver in his breast pocket as heavy as his heart, nearly sick with wonder and apprehension. The tropical suit he had been made to wear was monstrously hot, complete with full waistcoat and hard collar; the topee they insisted he use was as weighty as a crown. As he came in sight of the house, he could hear the awesome cries from the lion house, where the cats were evidently being given their dinner.

The big house appeared raw and unfinished to him, the trees yet ungrown and the great masses of scentless flowers—hydrangea, bougainvillaea, canna—that had smothered the place when last he had seen it, some decades later, just beginning to spread.

"Rhodes himself met me at the door—actually he happened to be going out for his afternoon ride—and welcomed me," he said. "I think the most striking thing about Cecil Rhodes, and it hasn't been noticed much, was his utter lack of airs. He was the least self-conscious man I have ever known; he did many things for effect, but he was himself entirely single: as whole as an egg, as the old French used to say.

" 'The house is yours,' he said to me. 'Use it as you like. We don't dress for dinner, as a rule; too many of the guests would be taken short, you see. Now some of the fellows are playing croquet in the Great Hall. Pay them no mind.'

"I remember little of that evening. I wandered the house: the great skins of animals, the heavy beams of teak, the brass chandeliers. I looked into the library, full of the specially transcribed and bound classics that Rhodes had ordered by the yard from Hatchard's: all the authorities that Gibbon had consulted in writing the *Decline and Fall.* All of them: that had been Rhodes's order.

"Dinner was a long and casual affair, entirely male—Rhodes had not even any female servants in the house. There was much toasting and hilarity about the successful march into Matabeleland, and the foundation of a fort, which news had only come that week; but Rhodes seemed quiet at the table's head, even melancholy: many of his closest comrades were gone with the expeditionary column, and he seemed to miss them. I do remember that at one point the conversation turned to America. Rhodes contended—no one disputed him

127

—that if we (he meant the Empire, of course) had not lost America, the peace of the world could have been secured forever. 'Forever,' he said. 'Perpetual Peace.' And his pale opaque eyes were moist.

"How I comported myself at table—how I joined the talk, how I kept up conversations on topics quite unfamiliar to me—none of that do I recall. It helped that I was supposed to have been only recently arrived in Africa: though one of Rhodes's band of merry men looked suspiciously at my sun-browned hands when I said so.

"As soon as I could after dinner, I escaped from the fearsome horseplay that began to develop among those left awake. I pleaded a touch of sun and was shown to my room. I took off the hateful collar and tie (not without difficulty) and lay on the bed otherwise fully clothed, alert and horribly alone. Perhaps you can imagine my thoughts."

"No," I said. "I don't think I can."

"No. Well. No matter. I must have slept at last; it seemed to be after midnight when I opened my eyes and saw Rhodes standing in the doorway, a candlestick in his hand.

" 'Asleep?' he asked softly.

" 'No,' I answered. 'Awake.'

" 'Can't sleep either,' he said. 'Never do, much.' He ventured another step into the room. 'You ought to come out, see the sky,' he said. 'Quite spectacular. As long as you're up.'

"I rose and followed him. He was without his coat and collar; I noticed he wore carpet slippers. One button of his wide braces was undone; I had the urge to button it for him. Pale starlight fell in blocks across the black and white tiles of the hall, and the huge heads of beasts were mobile in the candlelight as we passed. I murmured something about the grandness of his house.

" 'I told my architect,' Rhodes answered. 'I said I wanted

the big and simple—the barbaric, if you like.' The candle flame danced before him. 'Simple. The truth is always simple.'

"The chessboard tiles of the hall continued out through the wide doors onto the veranda—the *stoep* as the old Dutch called it. At the frontier of the *stoep* great pillars divided the night into panels filled with clustered stars, thick and near as vine blossoms. From far off came a long cry as of pain: a lion, awake.

"Rhodes leaned on the parapet, looking into the mystery of the sloping lawns beyond the *stoep*. 'That's good news, about the chaps up in Matabeleland,' he said a little wistfully.

"'Yes.'

"'Pray God they'll all be safe.'

"'Yes.'

"'*Zambesia,*' he said after a moment. "What d'you think of that?'

"'I beg your pardon?'

"'As a name. For this country we'll be building. *Beyond the Zambesi,* you see.'

"'It's a fine name.'

"He fell silent a time. A pale, powdery light filled the sky: false dawn. 'They shall say, in London,' he said, ' "Rhodes has taken for the Empire a country larger than Europe, at not a sixpence of cost to us, and we shall have that, and Rhodes shall have six feet by four feet." '

"He said this without bitterness, and turned from the parapet to face me. The Webley was pointed toward him. I had rested my (trembling) right hand on my left forearm, held up before me.

"'Why, what on earth,' he said.

"'Look,' I said.

"Drawing his look slowly away from me, he turned again. Out in the lawn, seeming in that illusory light to be but a long leap away, a male lion stood unmoving.

" 'The pistol won't stop him,' I said, 'but it will deflect him. If you will go calmly through the door behind me, I'll follow.'

"Rhodes backed away from the rail, and without haste or panic turned and walked past me into the house. The lion, ocher in the blue night, regarded him with a lion's expression, at once aloof and concerned, and returned his look to me. I thought I smelled him. Then I saw movement in the young trees beyond. I thought for a moment that my lion must be an illusion, or a dream, for he took no notice of these sounds— the crush of a twig, a soft voice—but at length he did turn his eyes from me to them. I could see the dim figure of a gamekeeper in a wide-awake hat, carrying a rifle, and Negroes with nets and poles: they were closing in carefully on the escapee. I stood for a moment longer, still poised to shoot, and then beat my own retreat into the house.

"Lights were being lit down the halls, voices calling: a lion does not appear on the lawn every night. Rhodes stood looking, not out the window, but at me. With deep embarrassment I clumsily pocketed the Webley (I knew what it had been given to me for, after all, even if he did not), and only then did I meet Rhodes's eyes.

"I shall never forget their expression, those pale eyes: a kind of exalted wonder, almost a species of adoration.

" 'That's twice now in one day,' he said, 'that you have kept me from harm. You must have been sent, that's all. I really believe you have been sent.'

"I stood before him staring, with a horror dawning in my heart such as, God willing, I shall never feel again. I knew, you see, what it meant that I had let slip the moment: that now I could not go back the way I had come. The world had opened for an instant, and I and my companions had gone down through it to this time and place; and now it had closed over me again, a seamless whole. I had no one and nothing; no Last equipment awaited me at the Mount Nelson Hotel; the Otherhood could not rescue me, for I had canceled it. I was entirely alone.

"Rhodes, of course, knew nothing of this. He crossed the hall to where I stood, with slow steps, almost reverently. He embraced me, a sudden great bear hug. And do you know what he did then?"

"What did he do?"

"He took me by the shoulders and held me at arm's length, and he insisted that I stay there with him. In effect, he offered me a job. For life, if I wanted it."

"What did you do?"

"I took it." He had finished his drink, and poured more. "I took it. You see, I simply had no place else to go."

Afternoon was late in the bungalow where we sat together, day hurried away with this tale. "I think," I said, "I shall have that drink now, if it's no trouble."

He rose and found a glass; he wiped the husk of a bug from it and filled it from his bottle. "It has always astonished me," he said, "how the mind, you know, can construct with lightning speed a reasonable, if quite mistaken, story to account for an essentially unreasonable event: I have had more than one occasion to observe this process.

"I was sure, instantly sure, that a lion which had escaped from Rhodes's lion house had appeared on the lawn at Groote Schuur just at the moment when I tried, but could not bring myself, to murder Cecil Rhodes. I can still see that cat in the pale light of predawn. And yet I cannot know if that is what happened, or if it is only what my mind has substituted for what did happen, which cannot be thought about.

"I am satisfied in my own mind—having had a lifetime to ponder it—that it cannot be possible for one to meet oneself on a trip into the past or future: that is a lie, invented by the

Otherhood to forestall its own extinction, which was however inevitable.

"But I dream, sometimes, that I am lying on the bed at
Groote Schuur, and a man enters—it is not Rhodes, but a man
in a black coat and a bowler hat, into whose face I look as into
a rotted mirror, who tells me impossible things.

"And I know that in fact there was no lion house at
Groote Schuur. Rhodes wanted one, and it was planned, but
it was never built."

In the summer of that year Rhodes—alive, alive-oh—
went on expedition up into Pondoland, seeking concessions
from an intransigent chief named Sicgau. Denys Winterset—
this one, telling me the tale—went with him.

"Rhodes took Sicgau out into a field of mealies where he
had had us set up a Maxim gun. Rhodes and the chief stood in
the sun for a moment, and then Rhodes gave a signal; we fired
the Maxim for a few seconds and mowed down much of the
field. The chief stood unmoving for a long moment after the
silence returned. Rhodes said to him softly: 'You see, this is
what will happen to you and all your warriors if you give us
any further trouble.'

"As a stratagem, that seemed to me both sporting and
thrifty. It worked, too. But we were later to use the Maxims
against men and not mealies. Rhodes knew that the Matabele
had finally to be suppressed, or the work of building a white
state north of the Zambezi would be hopeless. A way was
found to intervene in a quarrel the Matabele were having with
the Mashona, and in not too long we were at war with the
Matabele. They were terribly, terribly brave; they were, after
all, the first eleven in those parts, and they believed with
reason that no one could withstand their leaf-bladed spears. I
remember how they would come against the Maxims, and be
mown down like the mealies, and fall back, and muster for

another attack. Your heart sank; you prayed they would go away, but they would not. They came on again, to be cut down again. These puzzled, bewildered faces: I cannot forget them.

"And Christ, such drivel was written in the papers then, about the heroic stand of a few beleaguered South African police against so many battle-crazed natives! The only one who saw the truth was the author of that silly poem—Belloc, was it? You know—'Whatever happens, we have got/The Maxim gun, and they have not.' It was as simple as that. The truth, Rhodes said, is always simple."

He took out a large pocket-handkerchief and mopped his face and his eyes; no doubt it was hot, but it seemed to me that he wept. Tears, idle tears.

"I met Dr. Jameson during the Matabele campaign," he continued. "Leander Starr Jameson. I think I have never met a man—and I have met many wicked and twisted ones—whom I have loathed so completely and so instantly. I had hardly heard of him, of course; he was already dead and unknown in this year as it had occurred in my former past, the only version of these events I knew. Jameson was a great lover of the Maxim; he took several along on the raid he made into the Transvaal in 1896, the raid that would eventually lead to war with the Boers, destroy Rhodes's credit, and begin the end of Empire: so I have come to see it. The fool.

"I took no part in that war, thank God. I went north to help put the railroad through: Cape-to-Cairo." He smiled, seemed almost about to laugh, but did not; only mopped his face again. It was as though I were interrogating him, and he were telling me all this under the threat of the rubber truncheon or the rack. I wanted him to stop, frankly; only I dared say nothing.

"I made up for a lack of engineering expertise by my very uncertain knowledge of where and how, one day, the road would run. The telegraph had already reached Uganda; next stop was Wadi Halfa. The rails would not go through so easily. I became a sort of scout, leading the advance parties, dealing with the chieftains. The Maxim went with me, of course. I learned the weapon well."

Here there came another silence, another inward struggle to continue. I was left to picture what he did not say: *That which I did I should not have done; that which I should have done I did not do.*

"Rhodes gave five thousand pounds to the Liberal party to persuade them not to abandon Egypt: for there his railroad must be hooked to the sea. But then of course came the end of the whole scheme in German Tanganyika: no Cape-to-Cairo road. Germany was growing great in the world; the Germans wanted to have an Empire of their own. It finished Rhodes.

"By that time I was a railroad expert. The nonexistent Uganda Railroad was happy to acquire my services: I had a reputation, among the blacks, you see . . . I think there was a death for every mile of that road as it went through the jungle to the coast: rinderpest, fever, Nanda raids. We would now and then hang a captured Nanda warrior from the telegraph poles, to discourage the others. By the time the rails reached Mombasa, I was an old man; and Cecil Rhodes was dead."

He died of his old heart condition, the condition that had brought him out to Africa in the first place. He couldn't breathe in the awful heat of that summer of 1902, the worst anyone could remember; he wandered from room to room at Groote Schuur, trying to catch his breath. He lay in the darkened drawing room and could not breathe. They took him down to his cottage by the sea, and put ice between the ceiling and the iron roof to cool it; all afternoon the punkahs spooned the air. Then, suddenly, he decided to go to England.

April was there: April showers. A cold spring: it seemed that could heal him. So a cabin was fitted out for him aboard a P&O liner, with electric fans and refrigerating pipes and oxygen tanks.

He died on the day he was to sail. He was buried at that place on the Matopos, the place he had chosen himself; buried facing north.

"He wanted the heroes of the Matabele campaign to be buried there with him. I could be one, if I chose; only I think my name would not be found among the register of those who fought. I think my name does not appear at all in history: not in the books of the Uganda Railroad, not in the register of the Mount Nelson Hotel for 1893. I have never had the courage to look."

I could not understand this, though it sent a cold shudder between my shoulder blades. The Original Situation, he explained, could not be returned to; but it could be restored, as those events that the Otherhood brought about were one by one come upon in time, and then not brought about. And as the Original Situation was second by second restored, the whole of his adventure in the past was continually worn away into nonbeing, and a new future replaced his old past ahead of him.

"You must imagine how it has been for me," he said, his voice now a whisper from exertion and grief. "To everyone else it seemed only that time went on—history—the march of events. But to me it has been otherwise. It has been the reverse of the nightmare from which you wake in a sweat of relief to find that the awful disaster has not occurred, the fatal step was not taken: for I have seen the real world gradually replaced by this other, nightmare world, which everyone else assumes is real, until nothing in past or present is as I knew it to be; until I am like the servant in Job: *I only am escaped to tell thee.*"

* * *

March 8, 1983

I awoke again this morning from the dream of the forest in the sea: a dream without people or events in it, or anything whatever except the gigantic dendrites, vast masses of pale leaves, and the tideless waters, light and sunshot toward the surface, darkening to impenetrability down below. It seemed there were schools of fish, or flocks of birds, in the leaves, something that faintly disturbed them, now and then; otherwise, stillness.

No matter that orthogonal logic refutes it, I cannot help believing that my present succeeds in time the other presents and futures that have gone into making it. I believe that as I grow older I come to incorporate the experiences I have had as an older man in pasts (and futures) now obsolete: as though in absolute time I continually catch up with myself in the imaginary times that fluoresce from it, gathering dreamlike memories of the lives I have lived therein. Somewhere God (I have come to believe in God; there was simply no existing otherwise) is keeping these universes in a row, and sees to it that they happen in succession, the most recently generated one last—and so felt to be last, no matter where along it I stand.

I remember, being now well past the age that he was then, the Uganda Railroad, the Nanda arrows, all the death.

I remember the shabby library and the coal fire, the encyclopedia in another orthography; the servant at the double doors.

I think that in the end, should I live long enough, I shall remember nothing but the forest in the sea. That is the terminus: complete strangeness that is at the same time utterly changeless; what cannot be becoming all that has ever been.

I took him out myself, in the end, abandoning my commission to do so, for there was no way that he could have crossed the border by himself, without papers, a nonexistent man. And it was just at that moment, as we motored up through the Sudan past Wadi Halfa, that the Anglo-French expeditionary force took Port Said. The Suez incident, that last hopeless spasm of Empire, was taking its inevitable course. Inevitable: I have not used the word before.

When we reached the Canal, the Israelis had already occupied the east bank. The airport at Ismailia was a shambles, the greater part of the Egyptian Air Force shot up, planes scattered in twisted attitudes like dead birds after a storm. We could find no plane to take us. *He* had gone desperately broody, wide-eyed and speechless, useless for anything. I felt as though in a dream where one is somehow saddled with an idiot brother one had not had before.

And yet it was only the confusion and mess that made my task possible at all, I suppose. There were so many semiofficial and unofficial British scurrying or loafing around Port Said when we entered the city that our passage was unremarked. We went through the smoke and dust of that famously squalid port like two ghosts—two ghosts progressing through a ghost city at the retreating edge of a ghost of empire. And the crunch of broken glass continually underfoot.

We went out on an old oiler attached to the retreating invasion fleet, which had been ordered home having accomplished nothing except, I suppose, the end of the British Empire in Africa. He stood on the oiler's boat deck and watched the city grow smaller and said nothing. But once he laughed, his dry, light laugh: it made me think of the noise that Homer says the dead make. I asked the reason.

"I was remembering the last time I went out of Africa," he said. "On a day much like this. Very much like this. This calm weather; this sea. Nothing else the same, though. Nothing else." He turned to me smiling, and toasted me with an imaginary glass. "The end of an era," he said.

* * *

March 10

My chronicle seems to be degenerating into a diary.

I note in the *Times* this morning the sale of the single known example of the 1856 magenta British Guiana, for a sum far smaller than was supposed to be its worth. Neither the names of the consortium that sold it nor the names of the buyers were made public. I see in my mind's eye a small, momentary fire.

I see now that there is no reason why this story should come last, no matter my feeling, no matter that in Africa he hoped it would. Indeed there is no reason why it should even fall last in this chronicling, nor why the world, the sad world in which it occurs, should be described as succeeding all others —it does not, any more than it precedes them. For the sake of a narrative only, perhaps; perhaps, like God, we cannot live without narrative.

I used to see him, infrequently, in the years after we both came back from Africa: he didn't die as quickly as we both supposed he would. He used to seek me out, in part to borrow a little money—he was living on the dole and on what he brought out of Africa, which was little enough. I stood him to tea now and then and listened to his stories. He'd appear at our appointed place in a napless British Warm, ill-fitting, as his eyeglasses and National Health false teeth were also. I imagine he was terribly lonely. I know he was.

I remember the last time we met, at a Lyons teashop near the Marble Arch. I'd left the Colonial Service, of course, under a cloud, and taken a position teaching at a crammer's in Holborn until something better came along (nothing ever did; I recently inherited the headmaster's chair at the same school; little has changed there over the decades but the general coloration of the students).

"This curious fancy haunts me," he said to me on that

occasion. "I picture the Fellows, all seated around the great table in the executive committee's dining room; only it is rather like Miss Havisham's, you know, in Dickens: the roast beef has long since gone foul, and the silver tarnished, and the draperies rotten; and the Fellows dead in their chairs, or mad, dust on their evening clothes, the port dried up in their glasses. Huntington. Davenant. The President *pro tem."*

He stirred sugar in his tea (he liked it horribly sweet; so, of course, do I). "It's not true, you know, that the Club stood somehow at a nexus of possibilities, amid multiplying realities. If that were so, then what the Fellows did would be trivial or monstrous or both: generating endless new universes just to see if they could get one to their liking. No: it is we, out here, who live in but one of innumerable possible worlds. In there, they were like a man standing at the north pole, whose only view, wherever he looks, is south: they looked out upon a single encompassing reality, which it was their opportunity— no, their duty, as they saw it—to make as happy as possible, as free from the calamities they knew of as they could make it.

"Well, they were limited people, more limited than their means to work good or evil. That which they did they should not have done. And yet what they hoped for us was not despicable. The calamities they saw were real. Anyone who could would try to save us from them: as a mother would pull her child, her foolish child, from the fire. They ought to be forgiven; they ought."

I walked with him up toward Hyde Park Corner. He walked now with agonizing slowness, as I will, too, one day; it was a rainy autumn Sunday, and his pains were severe. At Hyde Park Corner he stopped entirely, and I thought perhaps he could go no farther: but then I saw that he was studying the monument that stands there. He went closer to it, to read what was written on it.

I have myself more than once stopped before this neglected monument. It is a statue of the boy David, a memorial to the Machine Gun Corps, and was put up after the First World War. Some little thought must have gone into deciding how to memorialize that arm which had changed war forever; it seemed to require a religious sentiment, a quote from the Bible, and one was found. Beneath the naked boy are written words from Kings:

> *Saul has slain his thousands*
> *But David his tens of thousands.*

He stood in the rain, in his vast coat, looking down at these words, as though reading them over and over; and the faint rain that clung to his cheeks mingled with his tears:

> *Saul has slain his thousands*
> *But David his tens of thousands.*

I never saw him again after that day, and I did not seek for him: I think it unlikely he could have been found.

AFTERWORD

MUCH OF THE IMPULSE AND MANY OF THE DETAILS OF THE
preceding come from the second and third volumes of Jan
Morris's enthralling chronicle of the rise and decline of the
British Empire, *Pax Britannica* (1968) and *Farewell the Trum-
pets* (1978). I hope she will forgive the author the liberties he
has taken, and accept his gratitude for the many hours she has
allowed him to spend dawdling in a world more fantastical
than any he could himself invent.

The story of Rhodes's death and many details of his
character and conversation are taken from Sarah Gertrude
Millin's elegant and neglected biography *Cecil Rhodes* (London, 1933).

The story of Rhodes in Pondoland, along with much else
that was suggestive, comes from John Ellis's book *The Social
History of the Machine Gun* (1975).

For an introduction to that book, for his convincing anal-
ysis of the possibilities and limits of what I have called orthogonal logic, and in general for his infectious enthusiasm for
notions, the author's thanks to Bob Chasell (hi, Bob).

IN
BLUE

In Blue

THE ROUTE THEY TOOK EVERY MORNING FROM
their dormitory to the project's buildings took them
through very old parts of the city. They crossed a
square where weeds grew up between enormous paving
stones, a square so vast it could diminish even the long,
square-columned, monolithic buildings that bordered it. The
square was usually deserted and silent; not even the indige-
nous population of the city, descendants of those who had
built this square or at least of men and women who had
inhabited it when it was still a living place, ever came here
much. It was too open, too lifeless: or rather it had a life too
large, too intimidating; nothing could be done with it. The
new populations of the city, the squatters and refugees, also
rarely came here; probably most of them weren't even aware
of its existence.

Hare's group passed out of the square beneath an arch
the height of ten men and as thick as a room. Looking up as
they passed under it, Hare could see that the honeycomb
pattern of its vaulting was distorted deliberately to make the
arch seem even higher, even more intimidating than it was.
The hexagons high up, in the center of the arch, were actually

smaller than the ones on the sides, lower down; the circles inscribed inside the hexagons were really ovals, making the center of the curve of the arch seem to retreat into a space within itself, a space that could not exist, a space into which Hare's heart seemed to be drawn.

Then he had passed under the arch and moved on with the others.

Why had they done it that way? Every morning he wondered. Why had it occurred to anyone to expend so much ingenuity on a trick like that, who had then been willing to take the trouble to execute it? Slaves. But they must have been skilled nonetheless, and proud of their skills. The effort of it, the enterprise of it, at once oppressed and lightened him, drawing his mind apart.

He looked back, as he always did, to see the whole of it, and to study the band of letters that ran across the top. Each letter must have been a meter long; between the words there were diamond-shaped stops as large as a hand. But what were the words? What was the language? He tried to memorize the first few letters, as he always did, but as always by the time he reached work he would forget their exact shapes.

He turned away. One or two of the others had also glanced back, to see what it was that Hare looked at, but they couldn't see it, and looked curiously at Hare; the woman who worked beside him at the project smiled at him, enjoying his oddness. Hare returned the smile and looked ahead.

Farther on were narrow streets, and these, too, contained fragments of the ancient city, not ruins so much as antiquities in the process of being packed up in new construction. That the old cornerstones and bits of columned fronts were being preserved in this way was an illusion; the incremental plan for new housing, for places to put the thousands who were coming in from the countryside, made it necessary to squeeze modular units wherever Applications determined they could go, leaving the old disorder to be carted away later. Hare supposed it wouldn't be long before the gray boxes, which stacked to any height, which could be piled up anyhow wherever there was room, would spill out into the square, growing with the shy persistence of ivy, higgledy-piggledy, full of children, strung with lines of laundry and hung with gaudy hectoring posters in country dialects. In these streets the uniform units had already climbed above all but the tallest of the older buildings, their zigzag stairways like ivy's clutching roots.

Through the open doors of some units, Hare's group passing by could glimpse women at stoves, or nursing children; more often, though, doors and shutters would be quietly closed as the group passed, the faces that looked out suddenly occluded by a door. These country people were shy; if they found themselves observed, they would turn away, or even cover their faces with their hands. Had they used to do so in their old home places? Where Hare had grown up, people had been friendly and talkative. He thought it must be the city, the sight of strangers, cadre in Blue who had an uncertain but real control over their lives. When Hare's group came upon children playing in the labyrinthine streets, they would stop playing and withdraw into doorways or behind pillars, silent, their dark eyes large; they wouldn't come out though Hare's group waved and called to them.

It was a problem in figure-ground mechanics, Hare thought: that the cadre in Blue knew themselves to be the servants of masters, the people; but the people thought that the servants were their masters—and of course there were instances when the servants did seem to be directing the lives of their masters. It must be hard for them, Hare thought: the uniforms of Blue meant survival, food, shelter, help, and before them even the grownups were as shy as children offered sweets or kindnesses by great strangers.

But most of Hare's group had, like Hare, also come here from the country or from small towns, and also felt themselves to be displaced—perhaps that's why they smiled and waved at the elusive children of the altered streets, and why they talked little or in low voices as they walked through this many-layered necropolis where the living trod on the dead, who when they had lived had trod on other dead. Hare, in the city, felt for the first time sharply how many more dead there are than living.

The dead had carved in stone; the living wrote on paper. The long, bannerlike posters were everywhere, explaining, exhorting, encouraging: not only explaining how not to waste water, but why it was important that water not be wasted. Some were torn off in midsentence, by hands or wind; kindly teachers whose mouths were suddenly stopped.

"Look," Hare said to the woman who walked next to him. He read from a poster: " 'If you don't know how to read, begin learning now.' "

"Yes," the woman said. "There's a lot of illiteracy still."

She took the hand of the woman next to her, who smiled without looking at her. Hare said nothing.

☐

Hare's work at the project was the preparation of training manuals, introductory lessons in act-field theory and social calculus. Presently he was working on an introduction to coincidence magnitude calculations.

It was not difficult work; it was far less demanding than the work for which Hare had been trained, and for which he had shown such early promise in school, when it was thought that he might be one of those few who could alter the calculus that altered the lives of men and women. When he walked the long halls of the project building, he passed the open doors of rooms where men and women sat together, without tools beyond a terminal or a pad or without even those, men and women at work on that calculus; Hare, as he passed their doors, hearing their low voices or their laughter, could almost see the networks of their thought growing. If they caught sight of Hare, they might wave, for he had worked with some of them in these rooms and in rooms like these in other places. Then he passed on, through other rooms, meeting rooms and commissariats and the communications annex, to the cubicles where work like his was done. Beyond these cubicles lay the maintenance sheds, the shops and warehouses. Then that was the end. Hare, sitting down at his work station and turning on the dim light above it, wondered how long it would be before he was shifted that one last degree.

Not long, he thought. He wasn't sure he could even complete the manual he was working on in any form that could be submitted. And beyond the maintenance sheds, the shops and warehouses? Only the world that Hare's manuals taught about: life: the whole act-field. He would most likely go on moving, as he had moved, by degrees down from the highest realm of thought about it, to a mere place in it: or no place.

He opened the composer on his desk and retrieved the notes he had made the day before.

"Introduction. Definitions. Description of contents. Figure-ground mechanics a necessity for coincidence magnitude calculation. Probabilities and how they differ from coincidence magnitudes: example. Problems and strategies: synchronicity, self-reference paradoxes, etc. Conclude introduction: importance of coincidence magnitude calculation to the social calculus, importance of the calculus to act-field theory, importance of act-field theory to the Revolution."

He considered these notes for a long time. Then, keyed to the line about the difference between probabilities and coincidence magnitude, he wrote this:

"Example:

"It was once believed that no two snowflakes are exactly alike. More properly we can say that the probability of any two snowflakes' being exactly alike is very low. The fall, at the same moment, of two snowflakes that are exactly alike, and the fall of those two snowflakes on this word 'snowflake' that you are now reading, would be a coincidence of a probability so low as to be virtually incalculable.

"But the *magnitude* of the coincidence, if it were to be calculated by the methods you will learn here, would not be high.

"This is because coincidence magnitude is a function of *meaningfulness* as well as of probability. We know that only acts (as defined by the special and general act theories) can have meaningfulness; an act's meaningfulness is a function of its definition as an act, a definition made possible by the infinitesimal social calculus. An act bearing high meaningfulness and low probability generates a high coincidence magnitude. To calculate meaningfulness against probability, and thereby arrive at the magnitude of the coincidence, requires that coincidence magnitude calculation be operable within act-field theory as a *differential* social calculus.

"Act-field theory predicts the occurrence, within any given parameters of the field, of coincidences of a certain magnitude. It is said to *account for* these. The appearance within those parameters of coincidences greater in magnitude than the theory accounts for is a coincidence of implicitly high magnitude, generating its own parameters in another dimension, parameters calculable within the theory, which then *accounts for* the higher level of coincidence. The generation of such new parameters is called an *implicit spike,* and the process is itself *accounted for.*"

Here Hare's thought branched.

"Implicit spikes," he wrote, and then erased it.

"Act-field theory, then," he wrote, and erased that.

Whichever way his thought branched it seemed likely to take him to the tolstoy edge.

Once (Hare had no conception of how long ago, but long ago) they had thought that if the position and velocity and mass of every atom in the universe could be known, at some given moment, then the next moment and thus each succeeding moment could be predicted with certainty. Of course such complete knowledge could not be assembled, no computer could be built large enough to contain all the facts, or to calculate with them; but if they could be. And then they learned that the universe was not made like that at all, that only probabilities of states and events could ever be known with certainty, and that the very act of measuring and perceiving those probabilities entailed altering them. Some people (Hare had heard) had gone mad when this was proven, out of the awful loss of certainty, the loss even of the possibility of certainty. Others rejoiced: the loss of false certainty made real knowledge possible. The calculations began again, and were fruitful. The universe of events danced inexhaustibly, and the mind could dance with it, if it would.

And there had also been a time (the same time, perhaps, the same olden days) when people had thought that history might also be calculated: that if the weather and the size of harvests and the productivity of factories and the rate of invention and every other possible variable could be known, though it could not be, and every hurt every person had suffered, every belief or thought each one had—every man's position and mass and velocity—then it could be known with certainty why every event that happened had happened, and what would happen next.

But the human universe was no more like that than the universe of stars and stones. Such calculations would fail not because they were impossibly difficult but because no such certainties as were aimed at could possibly exist. It could not even be determined what units were to be measured—human acts—and where one stopped and another began. All conceivable plans for making the measurements met a mirror paradox, a self-reference, an infinite regression: the tolstoy edge.

But only give in to that; only rejoice in it; only be not surprised to find that the points plotted on your graphs make a figure like your own face, and the calculations begin again. And are fruitful: the special theory of acts, empty now of any concrete content, defines an act, the definition including the meaningful activity of looking for such a definition; the general theory defines their entrainments, heterarchies, and transformations. Act-field theory creates a virtually infinitely dimensional simplex for operating in, and the infinitesimal social calculus separates the inseparable, one act from another, dissolving in its simplicity the self-reference paradox as completely as the infinitesimal calculus in mathematics had dissolved the paradoxes of division that had plagued it for so long. And the social calculus makes possible the Revolution: once frozen before the infinite divisions of distance to be crossed before the target is reached, the Revolution now is loosed by the archer's fingers and leaps the distance into the unfigurable, ultimately unknowable heart of man.

And how could he, Hare, sitting here now, know all that, know it so well that when he was a boy he had in one tiny way added to it (some refinements of figure-ground mechanics for which he had won a prize in school), how could he sit here now before it and be unable to describe it? How could it ever make him afraid?

And yet he could not bring himself to continue.

He leaned back in his chair, which groaned beneath his weight. He pressed a key on the composer and held it down, and letter by letter his story about the snowflakes was removed from the screen.

☐

Hare sat at lunch with Dev, a woman of about his age. He didn't know her well, but she for some reason chose him to talk to. She ate little, and seemed to be full of a story she both wanted to tell and didn't want to tell, about a young friend of hers, and their friends, whom Hare didn't know. Hare listened, nodding, sympathetic, for the woman felt some grief, a grief that the story she told should have revealed; but the way she told it made it impossible to understand. She said "you know" several times, and "all that kind of thing," and waved her hand and shook her head as at a cloud of gnatlike complications that she could see in her story but couldn't or wouldn't describe. Hare lost the thread; there were too many "she's" in the story for him to remember which was which.

"So we all *did* go swimming," the woman said. "That night, by the bridge where there's the embankment. Well, I said I'd go. And then she said she and her new friend, the other one from the one she came with, the one she'd just met, didn't want to—but they said, Oh, come on, everybody needs to cool off. You know."

Hare was listening carefully now.

"So they all took their clothes off. And they're really very young." She laughed. "And, well. With *her* it never bothered me, but you know they can be so unkind, or no, not that, I just couldn't. I mean I'm too old really for those games they play, you know? Girls together, like in school. You get beyond that kind of thing. I laughed about it, you kids go ahead, I just like to watch, I'm an old grandma. And they just let me sit."

Hare put down his bowl. He was smiling, too, and nodding, as though sharing with the woman this amusing part of the story, where she'd tried to act her age with offhand grace; and trying to feel the other feeling that the woman felt: exclusion from happy comradeship, and jealousy; and trying also to transmute his own sudden strong feelings, by careful atten-

NOVELTY

tion to her, into sympathy. He shook his head, smiling at how life sometimes goes on.

"Kids," she said. "At that age you just don't care."

Hare wanted to ask: What did they do together in the water? But he could not have asked this and maintained his air of casual interest; and he thought that if she told him he would not understand her answer rightly anyway, because what the young women did together in the water would be three times masked from him: by their own young feelings, by the feelings of the woman who watched them from the bank, and worst of all, by the obstruction of his own feelings, so irrelevant to the young women in the water and what they did together, and yet so fierce.

"I know what you mean," he said, remembering a day in spring years ago, when he was at school.

The school Hare had gone to as a boy was built in the shape of a T. In one branch of the T the girls were taught by female teachers; in the other branch the boys were taught by men. Where the branches met, the corridor of Hare's part ended, crossed by the corridor of the girls' part running at right angles. Going from class to class, coming near this juncture, boys could watch the girls walking in their part: books under their arms, or held up before them, embraced in that way that girls so often held their books but boys for some reason never did; talking together in groups or walking singly. Glances and waves could be passed from one part to the other, and brief conversations held there. There was a gymnasium in the school—Hare could not remember now just how it attached to the body of the school building—where alternately through the day boys' and girls' exercise classes met; it could also be filled with folding chairs when visiting cadre came to lecture. For these events the boys used one half of the floor, and the girls the other, separated by a wide aisle.

On fine days, after they had had their lunch, older students who had permission from their teachers were allowed to walk outside for a while on a strip of pavement that ran before the wide back doors of this gymnasium, to talk and smoke cigarettes. There was a proctor to watch them, but he usually absented himself. These were good students; they were being given a taste of the sort of privileges cadre had, and that they themselves might someday have. The boys understood that, and talk was usually serious. On a burning spring day, a first summer afternoon, Hare was walking with three or four other boys, smoking and talking. They were all laughing too loud, because of the day, and the sun, and summer coming. Then—either blown open by a gust of wind because they hadn't been properly closed, or opened from within by someone on purpose to bring cool air into the hot gymnasium—the double doors of the gymnasium opened.

There was a girls' class in progress. A girl Hare knew slightly, a cheerful laughing girl, stood framed in the doorway, legs wide apart, hair lifted by the sudden inrush of air. She wore only a band across her breasts and a sort of strap around her waist and between her legs. She waved to Hare, surprised but unashamed. Beyond her, in the comparative darkness of the gymnasium, were the others in the class. There were mats laid out on the floor. Two girls on each mat were wrestling; some wore the same breast band that the girl standing in the doorway wore, some who didn't need them yet didn't. Those not wrestling stood to watch the others. Hare saw all this in a moment. The girls within shouted and laughed, the wrestlers stopped and looked, some of the girls ran to hide. Around Hare the boys were laughing. Hare only stood staring, become eyes, his heart become eyes, his hands and mouth become eyes. Then the girl pulled the doors shut with a boom.

The boys around Hare laughed together, pummeling each other and shouting in an access of energy, until the proctor came smiling to see what was up, what the joke was. Hare turned away from the closed doors, feeling an almost unbearable sense of loss and exclusion; feeling withered and desiccated within, made old, by loss.

Hare wanted to ask the woman Dev if that was what she had felt by the river, watching her friend and the other young women: that sense of loss and exclusion.

But it couldn't be. Because she had, once, herself been one of those girls on the mats, among others. She had always been in the other part. The young woman swimming with the others was her friend; they were all her friends. Hare couldn't imagine then what she felt, whether her feelings were of the same kind as his, or a different kind altogether, and whether it hurt as much, or more, or less: her loss of what he had never had.

"I know what you mean," he said again.

□

Willy said to him: "You look tired. You always look tired now. You look as though someone knew something terrible about you, and you were afraid he was going to tell all your friends, and you can't stop worrying about it. But I know everything about you, and there isn't anything terrible at all."

Willy shared Hare's room in the dormitory building where the project staff were housed. Willy wasn't exactly cadre, he hadn't much education, he was good with his hands and worked in the project maintenance shops. But Hare, when he saw that he wouldn't be able to have a room of his own because the project staff had grown too large, had got Willy into his room. Willy didn't mind living with project cadre, he had no sense of inferiority, and everybody liked Willy, his goodness, his jokes, his sympathy with everyone. Willy got along.

Though they had often lost touch in the intervening years, Hare had known Willy since school. Willy was four years younger than he, and at summer work-camp when Hare was proctor, Willy, alone and unhappy at his first camp, had adopted Hare to be his friend and protector. He'd sneak out of his own bunk with the young children and make his way to Hare's bed, shyly but insistently climbing in with him. Hare, half asleep, didn't resist the boy's affection; he was embarrassed to find him there in the morning, as immovable as a log in his deep childish sleep, and the other proctors made fun of him, but they were jealous, too, that Hare had someone so devoted, to run errands for him; once there had been a fight with another proctor over Willy. Willy understood—he always understood the context, the human net of desires and fears, the act-field, in a concrete way that Hare never would—and after that when he crept into bed in Hare's cubicle, he would be silent; would lie with Hare almost not moving, and with his face pressed into the hollow of Hare's shoulder would masturbate him with small motions, sometimes seeming to fall asleep amid it. When Hare made noises, Willy would whisper *shhh* in his ear, and giggle.

Willy called it playing. He always did. It was more intense pleasure than eating, without that daily compulsion but no less automatic; as refreshing as football or hard calisthenics, but imbued with affection and intimacy. The continuum in Willy from simple affection and shared good times to those cryings-out, those spasms, was unbroken; it had no parts; it was the social calculus in reality, and Hare loved it in Willy and envied him for it.

Because for all he, Hare, knew the integral social calculus, in him there was such a division. There was a breaking into parts, as in the oldest and wrongest paradoxes; an infinite number of discrete distances to cross between himself and what he desired.

"It's because I want the other," he told Willy when long

ago he'd tried to say it in words. "You want the same. So it wouldn't occur to you."

"That's not it," Willy said, laughing. "Because I've been with women, too. I bet more than you have. I like people, that's the difference. You have to like people. If you like people, they'll like you back. Men or women. If you're interested in them, they like you for it. It's simple."

Hare had laughed, too, shame-faced, uneasy with the humility he had to learn in order to take advice from the boy whom he'd protected and taught. Pride: it was a fault cadre were liable to, he knew, a fault that must be erased. Why shouldn't he take advice from Willy? While Hare had grown up in the thin atmosphere of schools, study camps, and project dormitories, Willy had been moving in the sea of the people, the endless flux of the Revolution, with all its accidents and coincidences. Never cease learning from the people: that was a maxim of the Revolution grown old and unfeelable for Hare.

But he had tried to learn. He had tried to meld himself with the common play of desire and pleasure, hope and disappointment, pleasure and work. He became, or seemed to become, wise; became someone to whom others told stories, because of his calm, sensible sympathies. The endless voices: Hare heard stories everywhere, people told him of their plans and desires, Hare nodded and said *I know what you mean.*

But he had no stories himself that he could tell.

□

The dormitories where the cadre that worked in Hare's project lived were modular, like the people's housing, though the units were smaller. Above the communal facilities, the refectories and common rooms and work stations, the units were bolted on seemingly at random; but in fact Applications worked and reworked the building's program to assure that every unit got as much sun and air, as many windows, as short a walk to toilets, as possible; and so optimized along many dimensions it accreted as complexly and organically as a coral reef, and with the same stochastic logic.

Toward the summer's end the man who had lived alone in the unit next to Hare and Willy was shifted to another project. The people associated with his part in the project gave him a farewell party in one of the common rooms. They gave him a few small gifts, mostly jokes relating to work, and they ate cakes and drank tea spiked with some alcohol someone had got from the dispensary. Willy, to whom things like this were important, who remembered the birthdays of many people, had spent some time decorating the corner of the room where they sat, and he gave the departing man a real gift, an antiquity he'd found somewhere in the city and made a box for in the shop. The antiquity, a small white-enameled cube of thin metal, had a little door in the front that opened to show an interior space, and four red spirals symmetrically painted on its top, and representations of dials or knobs here and there. It was passed from hand to hand, everyone marveling at how old it must be and wondering what it might have been for. Willy was pleased with the effect. The man who was leaving was very touched, even surprised, Hare thought, and embraced Willy; and then, somewhat clumsily, all the others. Then the party was over.

The next week two young women came to live together in the empty room.

They were young, in training in the project, and inseparable; shy amid new people, but making their way together. Hare talked with them now and then when he found himself opposite them at dinner. They weren't sisters, though they looked enough alike to be sisters: both dark, with luminous eyes and full, childlike yet maturely sensual faces. Their light clothes of Blue (they had come up from a project in the south) revealed them as though without their knowledge or consent. They had a funny way of finishing each other's sentences. When Hare came upon one of them alone and began a conversation with her, she talked of little but her friend, her opinions and feelings, and kept looking around to see if she had come. When at last her friend appeared, a calm joy transformed her face. Hare watched her, his polite smile stuck on his face: watched love come and settle on her features and in the repose of her body.

Because they lived next to him, because he could hear through the thin wall the indistinct murmur of their voices and the sounds of their movements, Hare thought often about the two of them. The time he spent alone in his room was punctuated by the small sounds they made: a laugh over some joke Hare couldn't hear; obscure sounds of things moved or handled. Without willing it, he found himself growing alert to these sounds, his attention pricking up at them like a dog's ears. When Willy was also in the room, Hare paid no attention to the next room; his and Willy's noises drowned them out. But alone he listened; even held still to listen, found himself making the silent movements of a spy with his glass or his book, so as not to miss—What? he asked himself; and went on listening.

There was a night when loud scrapings, sounds of effort, laughter, business, went on some time next door; something bumped against Hare's wall. He could make nothing of all this until, after general lights-out, he climbed into bed and heard, close by him and more distinctly than before, the sound of their voices, the jounce and squeak of their bed.

They had shifted the few furnishings of their room, and moved the bed they shared from the far side of the room up against the wall that divided their room from Hare's, the same wall against which his own bed was placed. It was as though the three of them were now in the same bed, with the thin wall between them dividing it in two.

Hare lay still. There were long silences; a word from one of the two of them, a brief answer; the noise of the bed when one of them moved. He heard one of them get up, the pat of her naked feet on the floor; she returned, the bed spoke. With slow care he rolled over in his bed so that he lay next to the wall. Still he could hear no intelligible voices, only the sounds of their speech. But now, with the lights out, alone next to them close enough to touch them but for the wall, he knew he must hear, hear it all.

His mouth was dry, and there was a kind of intense constriction in him. Where had he once heard that you could eavesdrop on an adjoining room by putting a glass against the wall, and listening as though to a megaphone? He only thought about this for a time, lying still; then he slid from the bed, lit his night-light, and took his glass from the sink. His knees were watery-weak. The feelings he felt didn't seem to him to be sexual, weren't like the feelings caused by sexual fantasies, they were more dangerous somehow than that; and yet he knew now what he wanted to hear. He got silently back into bed; he placed the glass against the wall, and his ear against the glass, his heart beating slow and hard.

There was a sort of roar, like the sound of the sea in a shell, the sound of his own blood rushing; then one of the two women spoke. She said: "When the first boy has passed the last marker."

"All right," said the other. "I don't know."

Silence.

What were they talking about? They were together, in bed. Lights were out. They might still have a night-light on: that he couldn't tell. He waited.

"Last boy passes the first marker . . . ," said the second who spoke.

"No," said the first, laughing. *"First* boy passes the *last* marker. You got the last boy."

More silence. Their voices were distinct, and not far away, but still remote, as though they spoke from the bottom of a clear pool. Hare knew he could listen all night long, but at the same time he grew horribly impatient. He wanted a sign.

"I don't like that one. Let's do another."

"You're just lazy. Listen again."

"Oh, let's stop."

Hare understood then. They were solving a puzzle, the kind printed in the back pages of mathematical journals. Aimlessly, without paying it much attention, they were working out a relay-race problem. Hare did them himself sometimes, when he had nothing better to do.

How could that be? They had one another, they were alone in a room, in a bed, they loved each other, they were free, free together in circumstances so enviable that desire only to be a witness of it, only to know a little of it, had driven Hare to this shameful contrivance, the glass against the wall, the wanting ear against the glass: and they were working out —or not even really bothering to work out—a puzzle in a magazine. But why would they? How could they?

He lowered the glass from the wall. Desire must not be what he thought it was: if its satisfaction was always present, it must grow blunted, it must not even be often thought of. That must be so. If you lived with the one you loved you did puzzles, had arguments, sometimes made love, slept. Couldn't he have supposed that to be so? It was obvious. Desire was a wholer, though not a larger, thing than the thing that was within himself. Of course it must be: and that cut him more deeply than anything he had expected to overhear.

There was further talk from the next room. He picked up the glass and listened again, willing them to show each other love, for his sake. But the talk was unintelligible to him now, private, or perhaps directed at something visible to them alone: anyway, meaningless. Then speech grew infrequent. Still he listened. Then, when silence had gone on so long that it might as well have been an empty room he listened to, he gave up, exhausted by the effort of attention; no doubt they slept.

Hare didn't sleep. He lay awake, feeling irremediably cheated, cheated of their desire. He wouldn't have minded the hurt he would have suffered that their desire faced away from him, so long as he could have witnessed it; yet even that they had withheld from him—not even on purpose, not conscious of him at all, having no intention toward him whatever.

On other nights he listened again. He sometimes heard things he could interpret as lovemaking if he chose to, but nothing clear enough to gain him what he wanted—entrance, commonality, whatever it was. When he slept with Willy, he made a joke of it, telling Willy in a whisper that the two could be heard; Willy smiled, intrigued for a minute, then bored when nothing immediately amusing could be heard; then he slept. Desire kept Hare awake beside him. Desire lay heavily in him: his own, the two women's desire that faced away from him. Desire seemed lodged hard in his throat and gut, distorting his nature and his natural goodness, something foreign, not a part of him, which yet cut every part of him, like a knife he had swallowed.

That month when Willy was moved to the night shift and Hare saw him only at dinner and for a few moments when Hare was preparing to leave for the project and Willy had just returned, Hare felt a certain relief. He couldn't have stopped, now, listening to the undersea sounds that came through his drinking glass, and of course he couldn't do it when Willy was present—but it was more than that. He couldn't have put Willy out of his room, that would have been like cutting a lifeline, but he couldn't now have him nearby either. His presence was like a reproach, a sign that what had become of Hare need not have happened.

□

History no longer existed. Hare had had to reinvent it.

On his free days he would find excuses to avoid the communal activities of the dormitory, the classes and criticism sessions and open committee meetings, and with a tablet and pencil he would wander in old parts of the city, working and dreaming—working by dreaming—over this invention of his, history.

On a bench in a crowded park he sat opposite a great and now unused building, fronted with fluted pillars and crowned in the middle of its roofline with complex statuary, a group of men and women victorious or defeated, winged infants, and horses, which seemed to be bursting out of the unknowable old interior into the air of the present.

The building was a favorite of his, partly because it was still whole, partly because the present had not been able to think of a use for it, but mostly because as he sat before it— closing one eye, then the other, measuring with his thumb and with lengths of the pencil held up before him—he saw most clearly the one sure fact he had learned about the past. The past thought in geometry: in circles, sections of circles, right triangles, squares, sections of squares. The building before him was nothing but an agglomerate of regular geometrical figures, cut in stone and overlaid with these striving figures continually trying, but never succeeding, in bursting them apart. He imagined that the whole structure—even the fluting of the pillars, the relation of different bits of molding to one another—could be expressed in a few angles, in small whole numbers and regular fractions. Even the statues, with their wild gestures and swirling draperies, were arranged in a simple rhythm, a graspable hierarchy.

He thought it was odd that it should be so; and he

thought it was odd that he should derive so much pleasure from it.

Why had the past thought that the world, life, should be pressed into the most abstract and unliving of shapes—the regular geometrical solids that were foreign to all human experience? Except for a few crystals, Hare thought there were no such things in the world. The mind contained no such shapes; the shapes the mind contained, if they were to be projected into the world, would look like—they *did* look like —the clusters of people's housing that crept up to the edges of this park. They would look like the stacked, irregular dormitories Hare had lived in for years, restless accumulations always seeking optima, the result of a constant search amid shifting variables. Those were the mind's shapes, because the computers that designed the dormitories and the people's housing contained and used the logic of the mind: contained it so completely that the shapes that lay within the human mind, truly there in the resulting structures, were no more immediately apparent there than the shapes of the mind are in a casual conversation, with all its strategies, accommodations, distributions, and feedback loops.

But this building was part of the past. The past wasn't like the present. The past hadn't understood the shapes the mind naturally contained, it had no way of ascertaining them—no mirror as the present had in its big, linked computers; the past had longed for absolutes, for regularities foreign to the mind's nature, and (if the stories Hare had heard were true) had enforced them brutally on a heterarchical world. What peace, then, when all those hierarchies, when the very striving for hierarchy itself, had been dissolved in the Revolution! Peace; Perpetual Peace. The false and hurtful geometries had bent and melted and yielded to the unpredictable, immense stochastic flow of the act-field, leaving only a few memorials like this building, obdurate things caught in the throat of time.

Afternoon sunlight fell slantwise across the broad face, coloring its gray stone pink. There was a band of tall letters, Hare saw, running across the whole length of it, obscured by dirt: the light had cleansed them for a moment, and Hare, with many glances from his tablet to the building, copied them:

* IAM * REDIT * ET * VIRGO * REDEUNT * SATURNIA * REGNA *

He closed his tablet, and rose.

In the broad avenue that led away from the park and the building, people went by, an endless stream of them, bicycles and trucks, cadre in Blue, children and workers and country people. Two young women, one in shorts pedaling a bicycle, the other half-running beside her, holding with one hand the teetering bicycle that tried to match her slower pace. Both young, and smiling; they smiled at Hare when they saw that he watched them—happy, it seemed to him, and proud of their young health and beauty on a summer day. He smiled for them, paying them the compliment of being proud of it, too.

The people were a corrosive against all hierarchies.

Still smiling, Hare followed the avenue to where the cathedral stood on a square of its own. Its high doors stood open on this day; in winter they were closed, and only a small wicket let people in and out. And for whom had these immense doors been built, then, what beings needed such a space to go in and out by? As he passed through, he looked up at the ranked carvings of figures, human but attenuated and massed like a flight of birds, that swooped up the sides of the archway, ascending toward those seated at the top like a committee. Who were they all? The dead, he thought.

The interior of the church had been cleared of its benches. The great floor was being used (though vast spaces rose unused and useless overhead) as a clearing house for newcomers to the city. Groups of people stood before long tables waiting for housing and ration allocations. The sound of their footsteps, of the answers they gave to questions asked of them, even the taps of a pencil or the click of a terminal, rose into the upper volume of air and came to Hare's ears magnified and dislocated from their sources. Behind the tables low walls of board had been set up all along the stone walls of the church, whether to protect the walls, the windows and statuary, or simply for a place to pin up directions and information, Hare didn't know. He walked, head bent back, trying to follow the lines of the arches into the upper dimness. This, he thought, more than the other building across the park, mirrored the mind: the continual exfoliation of faces, birds, flowers, vines; the intersecting curves of vaulting, like the multiplane ellipsoids of a whole-program simplex; the virtually infinite reaching-away of it all into unseeable darkness. The colored, pictured glass, like the bright but immaterial reflections of the world in the thinking brain.

It wasn't so, though, really. His eyes, growing accustomed to the dimness, began to follow the lines of arches into the circles out of which they had been taken. He measured the regular spaces between pillars, and counted the repeated occurrences of squares, rectangles, triangulations, symmetries.

It was breathtaking how they had bent and tortured those simple ratios and figures into something that could approximate the mind. He felt a fierce joy in the attempt they had made, without understanding why they had made it. He thought this church must have been built later than the less complex but also somehow more joyful building beyond the park. He wondered if there was a way of finding out.

The low wall of flimsy board closed off some deep recesses even more full of figuration and glittering metalwork than the body of the church: like hollows of memory, if this were a mind, memory at once bright and dark. Peering into one such recess, Hare could see the statue of a woman atop a sort of table heaped up with what looked like gilt bushes. She wore robes of blue and a crown, a crown circled with pearls; some of the pearls had come out, leaving dark holes like caries. She stood beneath a little vaulted dome; a band of mosaic around the dome made letters, letters like those across the top of the arch he passed under every day, or the facade of the building down the avenue. He opened his tablet to a clean page and carefully copied the letters:

** A * V * E * E * V * A **

Ave Eva. "Ave Eva," he said aloud.

The woman's face—modest, with lowered eyes, despite her crown—did not look to Hare like the Eva he knew, his Eva. And yet he thought she did look, in her self-contained remoteness, a little like the Eva he sometimes dreamed of: dreams from which he would awake in a sweat of loneliness and cold loss.

He went out of the church.

No: now the building down the avenue, washed in sun, looked far the younger of the two, cheerful and new. Older or younger? He thought about it, blinking in the sunlight.

It seemed there ought to be enough of the past to make an act-field in itself; it rose vastly enough in Hare's mind, teasing him with limitless complexity. But it wasn't so. Even if everything that could be known about the past were known, it would still be far too thin to make an act-field. Even now, in order to construct a human act-field, the Revolution's computers ingested so much random matter that it was hard to find room in them for ordinary computations, food production, housing allocation: and even so, what the computers possessed was only a virtuality—a range of acts that was virtually but not truly infinite; enough for the Revolution's work, but still only a shadow cast by the immensity of the real act-field in which the people lived.

And history—out of which all old theories about society had been made—was a shadow of a shadow, so thin as to be for the program's purposes nonexistent. The whole of the past was less nutritious to the browsing search programs than the most meager meal of daily motions, truck accidents, school schedules, dew point, paper consumption, hospital discharges, decibel levels. The kinds of postulates that could be derived from history would not be recognized within act-field theory as postulates; out of the paucity of history, closed systems only could be constructed, those hurtful tautologies that ended in *ism,* once thrust onto the world like bars— systems less interesting than common arithmetic.

Hare knew all that. It didn't matter that the past was made of stone, and the present of thin walls of board bolted and stapled over it: history was a dream. History was Hare's dream. He didn't expect to learn from it; he knew better than that; he meant only to escape to it for a while.

Amid the crowds of the people; mounting up old stone steps, cut beside narrow cobbled streets; moving with the traffic along the broad avenues bordered with shuttered buildings; in the center of the great square, measuring its size by the diminution of a lone bicycle progressing toward the mouth of a far arch, Hare was in history, and his heart was calm for a while.

□

Hare wondered if the magnitude of the coincidence that had brought him together with Eva could be calculated, and if it were, what the magnitude would be. To daydream in that way meant to suspend his own knowledge of how such calculations worked—they could never work backward, they were abstracting and predictive; they could never calculate the magnitude of coincidences that had actually occurred. And Eva herself would have hated it that he should try to calculate her, predict her, account for her in any way.

Outlaw in a world without law, how had she come to be the way she was? Remembering the distances within her eyes, or waking from a dream of her regard turning away from him, he would think: she was trying to go far off. Loving Hare had not been a stopping or a staying but had been part of that going; and when he had explained to her that no, she couldn't go far off, didn't need to, and couldn't really even if she wanted to, then she went farther off by not loving him any longer—walking away, wearing her pregnancy like defiance, not hearing him call to her.

Hare sat at his desk at the project, looking at the notes for his manual on coincidence magnitude calculation, but thinking of Eva and the years since, years in which an automatic grasp he had once had of the Revolution's principles had weakened, a gap had opened between himself and his work, and the project that had been so eager to get him had begun to have difficulty finding something he could do. Eva had thought she could walk away from the world; Hare, standing still, had felt the world move away from him, grow less distinct, smaller.

No, that wasn't possible either. And any work he could do had its real importance to the Revolution, the same real importance as any other work; work for the Revolution had all the same formal properties and was all included; what it consisted of hour to hour didn't matter, it was all accounted for.

Importance of coincidence magnitude calculation to the social calculus. Importance of the calculus to act-field theory. Importance of act-field theory to the Revolution.

When Hare had been in school, that had been part of every lecture, on no matter what topic: its importance to the Revolution, its place in Revolutionary thought. Even in those days the boys hadn't listened closely; the Revolution was too old; it was either self-evident or meaningless to say that a thing was important to the Revolution, because there wasn't anything that was not the Revolution. *Dedicate yourself daily to the work of the Revolution,* said the tall letters that ran above the blackboards in his classroom. But that was like saying, Dedicate yourself to the activity of being alive: how could you do otherwise? If act-field theory, which lay at the heart of the Revolution and all its work, meant anything, then no act—no defiance of the Revolution, no grappling to oneself the principles of it, no ignoring or rejecting of it—could be not part of it. If any act could be not part of the Revolution, if any act could be conceived of as being not governed by act-field theory, then the field would dissolve; the Revolution would founder on the prediction paradox. But act-field theory was precisely the refutation of that paradox.

It was what he could not make Eva see. She was haunted by the thought that all her acts were somewhere, somehow, known in advance of her making them, as though the Revolution hunted her continually.

Importance of act-field theory to the Revolution. Hare twisted in his chair, linked his hands, changed the way his legs were crossed. The morning sped away.

There was a woman he had known in cadre training, at summer camp, in those days of night-long earnest conversations in screened wooden common-rooms, conversations that absorbed all the sudden feelings of young men and women for the first time thrust into daily contact. She had believed, or had told Hare she believed, that there was no such thing as act-field theory. She was sure, and argued it well, that for the Revolution to succeed, for the people to live within it happily and take up their burdens and do their work, it was only necessary for the people to believe that the theory *did* work. Once-upon-a-time, she said, social theories made predictions about behavior, and thus could be disproved or weakened or shown to be self-contradictory when behavior was not as the theory predicted, or when unwanted results arose when the theory was applied. But act-field theory simply said: whatever you do, whatever comes about in the whole act-field, is *by definition* what act-field theory predicts.

Every shocking or astonishing turn of events; every failed harvest, street riot, cadre shake-up; every accident or reversal in every life, are all as act-field theory says they must be. They are all accounted for, every spike, every rising curve, every collapse. And when the Revolution has swept away those failed and hurtful systems that attempt to predict and direct the future, there is nothing left to rebel against, nothing to complain of. There is Perpetual Peace. Street riots slacken in force, go unnoticed, are aberrations that have been accounted for even before they occur; the people go to work, harvests are steady, cadre do their jobs, there are no longer shake-ups and purges, none at least beyond those that have been accounted for. The Revolution is permanent. In the midst of its eternal mutability and changefulness, society no longer needs to change, or to hope for an end to change either. Life goes on; only the hierarchies are gone.

She said she didn't object to any of that. She felt herself to be in training precisely to do that work, to maintain the illusion that act-field theory governs human life in the same way that axioms govern a mathematical system. She felt (Hare remembered her uplifted face, almost aglow in the dark common-room, long after lights-out) that there could be no higher a task than to dedicate oneself to that work, which was cadre's work within the Revolution. Act-field theory dissolved social truisms like an acid, but it itself could never be dissolved; its works were its truth, the happiness of the world was its truth, the Revolution was its truth.

Hare listened, warmed by her certainty, by the strength of her thought; and he smiled, because he knew what she did not know. He had been where she couldn't go. She was no mathematician; she had not, as he had, just completed a multiplane ellipsoidal simplex and entered it onto the central virtual act-field and seen—he *saw* it, saw it like a landscape full of unceasing activity—the interior of the Revolution's data base, virtually as limitless as the actual act-field it reflected: and then saw it, at the bidding of his program, turn and look at itself.

How could he communicate that mystery? Ever since, as a schoolboy, he had learned that there are problems—in topology, in chaos description, in the projection of fractals— problems with true and verifiable solutions that only computers can construct, and only other computers verify, Hare had known how it was that computers could truly contain a virtual act-field, an image of the world larger than he could access within himself. He could put real questions about the world to the computers and receive real answers, answers not he nor any human mind could predict, answers only the computers themselves could prove true.

There *was* an act-field, and a theory by which it could be constructed. Just as Hare knew there was an interior in the young woman who sat beside him, which he could appre- hend through her words and through the strength of her thought touching him as he listened and looked, an interior bounded by the planes of her pale temples and the warm body real beneath her clothes of Blue, so he knew truth to be contained within the interiors of the Revolution's computers: truth both unbounded and boundless, endless by definition and somehow kind.

He remembered that feeling. He remembered it, but he no longer felt it. He could not ever, knowing what he knew, think as that woman had, that act-field theory was a lie or a kind of trick. He imagined, guiltily, what a relief it might be to think so, but he could not. But act-field theory no longer seemed to him kind, as it once had. It seemed to be hurting him, and on purpose.

But if act-field theory underlay the Revolution, and the Revolution could not hurt him or anyone, then act-field theory could not hurt him.

He sat back, his hands in his lap, unwilling to touch the keys of the composer, reasoning with himself—tempted to reason with himself, as a man with a wound is tempted to probe it, pull at the scab, pick at the hurt flesh.

He *did not need to feel* these things, he told himself. He did not need to write an introduction to his manual. It needed none. Of course any part of act-field theory could be introduced by an explanation of all of it, but no part *needed* such an introduction. The project knew that. Certainly the project knew that. In fact the project had given him this job precisely because it would not require him to think about the whole of act-field theory, but only about the simple mechanics of its application. And yet the fact that he could no longer think clearly about the whole (which was why he was here now before this antiquated composer) meant that when he was confronted with this simple introduction, he felt like a man confronted with a small symptom, not in itself terrible, not even worth considering, of a fatal systemic disease.

Perhaps, though, the project *had* thought of all that; perhaps it had put him here, in this cubicle, and presented him with the concrete, the explicit and fearful consequences of act-field theory, to punish him for no longer being able to think about the theory itself: for betraying, through no fault of his own, the Revolution. No fault of his own: and yet he felt it to be his fault.

No, that was insane. If the Revolution was not always kind, it was never vindictive, never; for a heterarchy to be vindictive was a contradiction in terms: the Revolution could not be if it could be vindictive.

Unless there was a flaw in the theory that underlay the Revolution, act-field theory, which made heterarchy in the world conceivable, which made the integral social calculus possible and therefore all the daily acts and motions of the human world, including his sitting here before his unwritable manual.

But there could be no flaw in act-field theory. Hare knew that as well as he knew that he was alive. Act-field theory proved that all possible disproofs of act-field theory were themselves provable parts of act-field theory, just as were all other acts. It was not even possible for Hare to consider act-field theory without the act of his considering having been accounted for by the theory.

All possible strategies for avoiding paradox within act-field theory were also parts of the theory; they were acts the theory defined. Just as his sitting here pursued by paradox was defined and accounted for.

Hare had entered into an infinite-regression fugue; the taste of infinity was in his mouth like metal. That which had freed the world held Hare like a vise, like a cell in which a madman runs eternally, beating his head first on one wall, then the other.

□

Hare got permission to go and visit Eva and his son in the country. It was never hard to get such permission, but it was often hard to find transportation for such a purely personal trip. Hare's cadre status was no help; in fact it was considered not quite right for cadre to be seen traveling for private reasons. It didn't look serious; it could seem like unearned privilege and might be offensive to the people. Hare learned of a convoy of trucks that was taking young people out of the city to help with the harvest, and he was promised a ride on one of these.

When Willy returned from his night shift, he shook Hare

awake, and as Hare, yawning and blinking, dressed, Willy undressed and climbed into the warmth Hare had left in the hollow of the bed. Hare went out into the empty, frosted streets, still tasting the dream from which Willy had awakened him.

Hare wondered if there were different names for different kinds of dream. This dream had been the kind where you seem to be telling a story to someone, and at the same time experiencing the story you are telling. Hare had been telling a story to Willy, a shameful and terrible secret that he had always kept from him, but which he had to confess to him now because Willy wanted to play. He had to confess how when he was a boy—and here he seemed not only to remember the episode but to experience it as well—when he was a boy, he had cut off his penis. He had done it deliberately, for what seemed like sufficient and even sensible reasons; he had kept the cut-off penis in a box. He saw himself opening the box in which he had kept it, and looking at it: it was erect but dead-looking, white, the veins in it pale. As he looked at it, the dream rising away from him, he realized how stupid he had been—how horribly stupid to have done this irrevocable thing that could never, ever be repaired, why, why had he done it—and as he contemplated the horror, Willy's hand awoke him. Relief of the purest kind washed over him, the dreadful burden fell away: it was all a dream, he hadn't done it at all. He grasped Willy's hand and laughed. Willy laughed, too. "Just a dream," Hare said.

Hare walked through the streets to the truck depot, shivering, feeling alternately the horror of the dream and the relief of waking. He had been distant with Willy lately: he ought to stop that, there was no reason for it.

Young men and women, students and younger cadre, filled the open trucks, mostly in Blue, mostly laughing and pleased at the prospect of a day in the country. Hare found the driver who had promised him a ride, and he was helped into the truck by several hands. The convoy started its engines, and as dawn threw long bars of sun between the buildings, they drove out of the city. The young people in Hare's truck began to sing, their strong high young voices clear, and the truck's engine a bass accompaniment to their song. It was stirring.

More somber, across the bridge, were the wide tracts of old city suburbs, long straight streets crossed by dirt roads where pools of water colored with oil stood in the truck ruts. Children, who perhaps belonged to the flowerets of modular housing growing over the dumps and shacks and abandoned factories, looked up to watch them pass. The young people stopped singing and began to find places within the truck's bed where they could sit comfortably through the long ride. Some opened books or journals they had brought. Some of the women lit cigarettes, though none of the men did.

Almost all the boys Hare had known who smoked cigarettes gave them up at a certain age, once out of school, but many women didn't. Women who smoked were of a certain kind, Hare thought; or at least they all seemed to roll and smoke their cigarettes in the same way, with the same set of gestures. Like that one, sitting with another out of the wind in the shelter of the cab: tall, lean, her hair cut short and carelessly, she used her cigarette in a curt, easy way, dangling it in her long hand that rested over her knee, flicking it now and then with her thumbnail. She rolled it within her fingers to lift it to her lips, drew deeply though it had grown almost too short to hold, and gracefully, forcefully, two-fingered it away over the truck's side, at the same time dismissing the smoke from herself through mouth and nostrils. The hard way she smoked seemed like the mark of a sisterhood; her friend beside her smoked in much the same way, though not tempered by the grace, the young eyes, or the kind smile that this one paid to Hare when she caught him studying her. Hare returned the smile, and the woman, still smiling, looked away, running her hand through her hair.

Hare laughed, enjoying the way what she did to mask herself, the smoking, revealed her to him. Young: when she was older, and more practiced, it wouldn't reveal her, but just now, in this morning, it did. Perched on the truck's scuppers, among youth—among the unmarked who desired so much to be marked, and in their desire, showing their tender just-born selfhoods the more cleanly, the more tartly to his senses—Hare for a moment felt how well after all the world is put together, and how well the people in it fit into it: a seamless act-field into which, no matter what fears he felt, Hare too fitted: into which even his fears of not fitting also fitted in the end.

He thought of Eva.

The truck left him off at a bare crossroads, where it turned toward the broad garden lands. He walked the two or three miles to the cadre crèche where Eva lived and worked, and where their son was growing up: three years old now. Hare had with him some books for Eva—she always complained there weren't enough, or the ones she could get weren't interesting—and a gift for his son, which Willy had made: a nesting set of the five regular geometric solids, all inside a sphere. They could be taken apart, and with some trouble, put back together again.

□

It had never been the case that anyone, any bureau or person or committee, ever forbade a marriage or some permanent arrangement between Eva and Hare. There was no committee or person who could have done that. Eva believed from the beginning, though, that such a barrier existed; it made her at once fearful and angry. Hare couldn't convince her that, whatever stories she may have heard, whatever rumors circulated, cadre weren't forbidden to regularize affairs like theirs. "They don't want it," Eva would say. "They don't care about anyone's happiness, so long as the work gets done. They never think about anything but the work." And Hare could not make her believe that, in the very nature of the Revolution, there was no "they," there could not be a "they" of the kind she feared and hated.

Certainly there was a tedious set of procedures that had to be gone through, but none of them were restrictive, Hare insisted, they were only informational. Many different people, yes, had to be informed; Hare and Eva's plans had to be passed outward into wider and wider circles of diffusion, first to the proctors and flow people at the project, then to the committee representatives at the dormitory, then the neighborhood and city committees; eventually the whole Applications system would have to be informed—would in the course of things become informed even if they only made their intentions known to the first levels of this diffusion. And it was true that in some ways they, Hare and Eva, would stick out: the two of them would make a spike within the regularities of cadre life, which was almost entirely unmarried, assumed to be celibate out of dedication and the pressure of work, and communal in ways that made strong pacts between individuals unusual; which meant that strong pacts between individuals upset people who were upset by unusual things. But why, Hare asked Eva, shouldn't the two of them be an oddity? Didn't she know that such oddities, such spikes, were implicit in the forms of communal life if that life isn't imposed by a hierarchy, is not tyrannical, is chosen, is the Revolution itself? They are assumed; they are already accounted for.

She did know that. But when Hare said—carefully, mildly, without insistence, a plan only for her to consider— that they could make their plans known at the first levels, within the first circles, and see if they were prevented even in the most subtle ways, and at the first signs of such resistance (though he knew there could be no such resistance) draw back if she liked: then she looked away and bit her nails (they were small, and bitten so short that the flesh of her fingertips folded over them; it hurt Hare to look at them) and said nothing.

She wanted something to defy, and there was nothing. She didn't want to hear his explanations of heterarchy, and when he made them, he felt as though he were betraying her.

He knew so much. He knew nothing.

He remembered her face, the day when she told him she was pregnant: her eyes questioning him even as her mouth said she didn't care what he did, this act was hers, she alone had decided on it. She expected some declaration from him, he knew: a denunciation of her for having done this, or a sudden pact offered that he would join her in it, as though joining a conspiracy. It didn't even seem to matter which he did—join her or denounce her. In fact he did neither, not being able to imagine either, not knowing why she should set such terms for him, yet knowing also that it was not really he who was being challenged; and obscurely certain he was failing her by not being able to feel as she did—that her act was a crossroads, a crux, a turning point where a fatal choice had to be made.

He thought: *What if I had pretended to understand?* If she thought she was surrounded by watching authorities, who wanted her not to do what she wanted, if the child had been a defiance of those authorities, then what if he had somehow pretended to join her in her defiance? Would she have believed him? Would she not have gone away? He thought it was possible, and it hollowed his chest to think so.

The cadre crèche was a cluster of low buildings, dormitories, a barn, yards, infirmary, school; beyond were the gardens and fields that the commune worked. In and out the doors, through the halls bright with autumn sunlight, boys and girls came and went, and women tending groups of children. Hare thought this must be a good place for children; it was crowded with the things children like—tools, growing things, farm animals, other children.

He wandered from room to room with his gift and books, asking for Eva. All the men and women who lived and worked in the crèche were parents of children being raised here, but many other children of cadre were here whose parents had chosen not to stay with them. Hare thought of them, the parents, separated also from each other perhaps, attached to faraway long-term projects, or working with the people in distant cities.

It's just hard for cadre, that's all, he thought, very hard. The people acted as they acted, their actions describable by theory but otherwise unbound; for cadre it was different. There were no *theoretical* barriers to their acting just as they would; theoretically, they did exactly that. In practice it was different, or seemed to be different; there seemed to be a gap there, a gap that only kindness and a little good humor could cross. He and Eva were bound by that now, if by nothing else; bound by what separated them, by the whole front of the Revolution sweeping forward at once, which could not be otherwise. With kindness and humor they could cross the gap. It was enough; no one had anything better. It was hard but fair.

In the summer refectory the long tables were now heaped with gourds and vegetables to be put by for the winter; men and women were stringing onions and peppers, hanging up bunches of corn to dry, packing potatoes for storage. Hare stood at the threshold of the broad, screened room filled with harvest, sensing Eva among them before he saw her.

"Hello, Eva."

She turned to find him behind her, and a smile broke on her face that lifted his heart as on a wave. "Hello," she said. "How did you get here?"

"I found a ride. How are you?"

She only regarded him, still smiling; her cheeks were blushed with summer sun, like fruit. "Where's Boy?" Hare asked.

She had called their son only "the boy" or "boy" from the start, refusing to give him any other name; eventually "Boy" had become simply his name, a name like any other.

"He's here," Eva said. She leaned to look under the table at which she sat and called: "Boy! Come see."

He came out from beneath the table, dark curls first, and lifted his enormous eyes (they seemed enormous to Hare) first to his mother, and then to Hare. "Hello," said Hare. "I've brought this for you."

He held out the sphere to Boy, without revealing its secret, and Boy took it from him cautiously; the length of his eyelashes, when his eyes were cast down to study the gift, seemed also extraordinary to Hare. He opened the sphere; inside it was the pyramidal tetrahedron.

"I sent a message," he said. "Didn't you get it?"

"No," she said. "I never go to the terminals. You haven't come to stay, have you?"

"No," he said. "No, of course not."

"You still have work, at the project?"

"Yes." If he had said no, would her face have darkened, or brightened? "It's not the same work."

"Oh."

She had done nothing since he had known her but pose questions he could not answer, problems without solutions; why then did he hunger for her as though for answers, the answers that might unburden him? All at once his throat constricted, and he thought he might sob; he looked quickly around himself, away from Eva. "And you?" he said. "What will you do now?"

Eva was coming near the end of her time at the crèche; she would soon have to decide what she would do next. She couldn't return to work on any of the major projects whose people were housed in the agglomerate dormitories such as Hare and Willy lived in. There were cadre who lived outside such places, among the people, but for the most part they did work for which Eva wasn't trained.

She could also ask to be released from cadre: put off her clothes of Blue and join the people, and live however she could, as they did. She and Boy.

"What will you do?" Hare said again, because she hadn't answered; perhaps she hadn't heard him. Eva only looked down at Boy absorbed in opening the tetrahedron. For a moment it seemed to Hare she resembled the statue of the crowned woman in the cathedral. Ave Eva.

"It might be," he said, "that they would have work for you here, if you asked for it. For another year or more. So that you could stay on here. Isn't that so?"

Boy had turned and stood between his mother's legs, lifting the tetrahedron to her, patient to be helped. Eva only laughed, and picked him up.

"Would you want to do that?" he asked. And just then Boy, in Eva's arms, reached out for him, gleefully, and clambered from his mother to Hare.

The first thing Hare perceived was the boy's weight, much greater than he had expected from the compact miniature body; yet heavy as he was he seemed to fit neatly within Hare's lap and the compass of his arms, as though they were made to go together—which they were, in a way, Hare thought. The second thing he perceived was Boy's odor, a subtle but penetrating odor that widened Hare's nostrils, an odor of skin in part and a sweetness Hare couldn't name. He could almost not resist thrusting his face into the crook of Boy's neck to drink it in.

Eva had begun to talk of her life at the crèche. It was tedious, she said, and every day was much like every other, but she had come to prefer it to the city. All summer, she said, she had worked in the gardens, learning the work with a man who had been a long time in the country, working with the people. He was someone who couldn't be predicted, she said, just as she was herself such a person; someone outside the predictions that were made for everyone, for every person. She had liked talking with him, hearing about other ways of life in other places, other possibilities; after work they had often gone walking with Boy, in the evenings that had seemed to her so huge and vacant here, quiet, as though waiting to be filled.

"As though you could step into them and keep walking away forever," she said.

"Yes."

"That's what he said."

"Yes." But Hare had not been listening; he had been hearing Boy, and feeling him, the solidity of him in his lap. He had begun to imagine what it would be like to live here, as Eva and Boy did. He thought of the passage of days, the work that there would be to do—work which Hare had never done but which he could just now imagine doing. *Have you come to stay?* Eva had asked him, as though it were possible he might. He was Boy's father, after all; he had a place here with him, too. Perhaps, if he did, if he came to stay with Eva and Boy, he might in the course of a year recover the balance he had lost, shake off the lethargy that bound him.

"Would you want to do that?" he asked again.

"Do what?"

"Stay here. If you could."

She looked at Hare as though he had said something not quite intelligible. "I'm not going to stay here," she said.

"Where are you going?" Hare asked.

"I'm going," Eva said. "They can't have me any longer."

"But where?" Hare insisted. "What city? What town? Are you going to look for another project? Are you going to give up Blue?"

She had begun to shake her head, easily but certainly rejecting each of these possibilities. It would not be, her face seemed to say, anything that could be predicted.

"Eva," Hare said. "You know you can't just . . . just fall out of the universe." He had begun to experience an awful swooning vertigo. "You can't, you can't. You'll be alone, you . . ."

"I won't be alone."

"What? What do you mean?"

"I told you," Eva said. "I told you about him. I was telling you all about him. Weren't you listening?"

"Oh," Hare said. "I see."

"You tell me there's no place to go. But there has to be."

"I didn't mean that. I meant—"

"There has to be," Eva said, looking away.

Hare sat still and said nothing further, but it seemed at that moment that the color began to be drained from everything that he looked at: the fruits and orange gourds on the tables, the people in Blue, the colored tiles of the floor. The boy he held, who had a moment ago seemed as large as himself, no, larger, seemed to grow small, distant within his arms, a foreign thing, something not connected to him at all, like a stone. He looked up. Had the sun gone behind clouds? No, it still shone. Where did this awful chill come from? "It's not what I meant," he said again, but did not hear himself speak it; he could only marvel at what had happened, what had happened and would not cease happening. Boy fell silent, and slipped out of his arms to the floor.

"I don't feel well," he said, and stood abruptly. "I'd better go."

Both Boy and Eva were looking at him, curious and not unkind, not kind either; not anything. Their faces were stones or closed doors, the faces of those at accidents or public quarrels. Hare thought he would see such faces if he were to die in the street.

"Do you want to go to the infirmary?" Eva asked.

"No. I'll go."

"Are you sure?"

"I'll go," Hare said. "I'll go. I'll go. I'll go."

□

He had thought it was just a story he was being told, about working in the gardens, about summer evenings, empty and vast. He hadn't listened carefully; he hadn't known that there would come this sickening reversal of figure and ground, showing him a story he had not suspected, that he was all unready for. Nothing had been as he thought it was; he had walked into what was the case as into a truck's path.

Hare stood at the crossroads awaiting the trucks returning from the farmlands to the city. The strange gray blindness that had afflicted him at the cadre crèche had not passed, nor had the dreadful stonelike weight in his chest. He patted his chest as he stood waiting, trying to press it down. He thought perhaps he would go to the infirmary when he returned.

It was true what he told her, though, what he knew about heterarchy and she did not, that it was limitless, that it could not be got outside of, that to think about it as though it had an inside and an outside was a kind of pain, the pain of error that is fruitless, unnecessary, because self-inflicted: this conviction that by choice or by some dreadful mistake it is possible to fall

out of the universe. Hare knew (it was all that he had ever tried to make her see) that it was not possible to fall out of the universe.

He thought of her and Boy and the man they were going away with. His thought followed them into a featureless stony landscape, without weather or air, under a vault of dun sky. Forever and ever would they be there.

He tried to draw breath deeply, but the painful bolus beneath his sternum seemed to prevent it; he could not get the air he needed.

Perhaps he would die. He wasn't old, but he seemed to be suffering some irreversible debility that quickened almost daily. He could not clearly remember, but he thought he had not really been well since the time when he was a boy and had cut off his penis.

No, that was a dream. Wasn't it? Yes, of course it was. With horror Hare realized that for some hours he had actually been assuming it to be so: that he had done such a thing and was now living with the consequences.

No. He wasn't truly ill. It was only this weather oppressing him, airless and chill, this close vault of dirty sky. He was grievously thirsty. Perhaps he would die.

The trucks surprised Hare, appearing suddenly past sundown; apparently he had been standing and waiting for hours without noticing time pass. He waved. The truck that stopped to pick him up was not the one that had brought him out; the young people who helped him in were not the same, were not the cheerful boys and girls who had sung children's songs and talked and laughed. These looked at Hare in silence, their faces in the twilight pale and reserved.

Hare thought he should explain himself to them. Perhaps he could ask them for help. He opened his mouth, but his throat was so dry and constricted that no words came out; he gaped foolishly, he supposed, but no one smiled. He forced his throat to open, and a gout of language came out that Hare did not intend or even understand.

He had better not talk more, he thought. He sought for a place to sit down; the silent young people drew away from him as he crept toward the shelter of the cab. He supposed that after all no one had heard the nonsense he had spoken, not over the noise of the truck's engine: an awful imploding roar that grew steadily worse, sucking the air from Hare's mouth and the thoughts from his head. He leaned against the cab, his hand hanging loosely over his knee; with his thumbnail he flicked the fragment of cigarette he held between his fingers. He was certain now that he would die of his old wound, or, far worse, that he would live forever. Forever and ever. "Ave Eva," he said, and a woman laughed. Hare laughed, too. The words seemed the only thing that could relieve his thirst. *Ave Eva,* he said again, or thought he said, unable any longer to hear himself under the withering roar. *Ave Eva. Ave Eva. Ave Eva. Ave Eva.*

□

The committee had high seats behind a long desk. This was not so that they sat above those who came before them to be examined—Hare's guard explained this to Hare—but so that everyone in the room could see them clearly. The committee leader had a seat on one side, and before her she had some dossiers and some things taken from Hare's room, including the sketches of old buildings and the attempts Hare had made to decipher their inscriptions. Hare found it hard to recognize these things; when the committee leader held up a sketch and asked Hare if he had made it, he couldn't answer. He tried to answer; he opened his mouth to answer, but could not make an answer come out.

The committee was patient. They listened to testimony about Hare, what he had done, how he had been found. They rested their cheeks in their hands, or they leaned back in their chairs with their hands folded in their laps; they asked gentle, unsurprised questions of the people who came before them, trying to get a clear story. When there seemed to be a contradiction, they would ask Hare what had happened. Hare opened his mouth to answer; he thought he could answer, possible answers occurred to him, then other possibilities, opening and branching like coincidence-magnitude calculations, switching figure and ground. Still he thought he could answer, if he could only say everything at once, describe or state the whole situation, the whole act-field, at once; but he could not, so he only struggled for a while with open mouth while the committee waited, watching him. Then they returned to questioning the others.

The two women who lived in the dormitory room next to Hare described how he had got into their room late at night: how he had forced his way in, though talking all the time very strangely and gently, about how he meant them no harm, wanted only to explain. They told (interrupting each other, finishing each other's sentences, until the committee head had to speak sharply to them) of their fear and confusion, of how they had tried to get out of the room, how Hare had prevented them. A torn nightdress was shown to the committee. The committee talked among themselves about attempted rape, asking questions that embarrassed the two women, but asking them so gently that answers were got at last.

Some others from the dormitory described how they had come to the women's room, and their struggle with Hare. They were eager to explain how or why it was that they had let Hare go, had not apprehended him and taken him then and there to security or to the committee representative. The committee head, not interested in hearing this, kept guiding the witnesses back to the facts of Hare's struggle: what weapons he had had, how he had behaved, what he had said.

Willy came in. He wanted to go and stand next to Hare, but the committee asked him to stand where the other witnesses had stood; and all through his story he kept looking at Hare, as though pleading with him to say something, to behave in some way that Willy understood. Hare saw that Willy's hands shook, and he wanted to take his hand, to say something to calm him, but he couldn't move. His guard sat behind him with his hands in his lap and probably wouldn't have prevented his going to Willy or speaking to him, Hare thought; but he couldn't do it, any more than he could answer the committee's questions.

Much of Willy's story was taken up with how tired and upset Hare had been before this incident, the bad dreams he had had, the troubles at the project. Hare couldn't remember any of the things Willy told about—any more than he could remember going into the women's room, or fighting with the people in the dormitory—but it seemed to him that the more that Willy, with every kind intention, tried to explain away Hare's behavior, the worse it looked to the committee. It sounded as if Willy knew something really terrible about Hare, and out of love was covering it up.

But Willy had once said to Hare that he knew all about him, and there wasn't anything terrible.

Hare wanted to say that, more in Willy's defense somehow than his own, but he could not.

Then, as Willy told about going out after Hare, and searching the city for him, Hare began to remember something of the events that were being told to the committee. In the same way that a dream that is forgotten on waking can be brought into the mind, disconnected but vivid, by some event of the day, some word or sight, Hare caught sight of bits of the story he had been in. When Willy told of finding him at last, huddled on the wide steps of the building whose inscription he had copied out, he remembered. Not how he had come to be there, or what had happened to him before, but that alone: Willy's hand on his shoulder, Willy's face before him, speaking to him. And he knew also, with a deep horror that deafened him to the committee's further proceedings, that that had not happened yesterday, or the day before, but weeks ago; and he remembered nothing at all of what had happened between then and now.

The committee leader was speaking, summing up the committee's findings. The case was really out of their provenance, she thought, and should probably not have been brought before the committee. She asked Hare if he had anything further to say.

The guard behind Hare leaned forward and tapped Hare's shoulder. Hare stood.

"Do you have anything you want to say?" the committee leader said again, patiently and without insistence.

"It's hard," Hare said. This came out of his mouth as though it were a stone he had dislodged from his throat, not like something he had decided to say. "It's very hard!"

He looked at the faces in the room, the committee, his neighbors, Willy. He knew, suddenly, that they would understand: they must, for they were all engaged with Hare in this hard thing together. "We all know how hard it is," he said. "The work of the Revolution. To grasp its principles isn't easy. To *live* them isn't easy. I've tried hard. We all have." They would understand how he had stumbled, they must; they would help him to rise. Together, in the face of the awful difficulties of the Revolution, they would go on. If he could lean on them, then as soon as he regained his feet, he could try again to be someone on whom others leaned. He smiled, and waited for their smile in return. "It's hard, always grappling with these difficulties. Act-field theory: that's hard to think about." He shook his head in self-deprecation. "Oh, I know. And the duties of cadre. The duty to *understand*. The committee knows how hard it is; everyone knows. I only want to say that I've tried. I want the committee to understand that. The committee understands. You understand."

He stopped talking. The circle of faces around him had not changed. It watched him with what seemed to him a terrible reserve, and something like pity. He knew he had not been recognized. He said, to the calm, closed face of the committee head: "Don't you think it's hard?"

"No," she said. "Frankly, I don't."

Frankly. Hare could not stand up any longer; his knees were unable to support him. Frankly. She had spoken with that remote, unmoved concern, the remote concern with which an adult will speak to a child in moral difficulties, difficulties the adult doesn't feel; without anger, with some impatience, without collusion: collusion would be inappropriate. Hare knew himself to be absolutely alone.

He had stopped speaking. After a moment the committee head gave the committee's resolution. Hare was to be remanded to a hospital. The committee head said she was sure that with rest and attention, Hare would return to normal. When he was better, they might have another meeting, and consider what amends Hare might be able to make for his behavior, if any were thought to be necessary then. Her last words to Hare were the usual formula spoken at the end of committee deliberations, when disposition of someone's case was made. She said: "Did you hear that?"

□

In the spring, discharged from the hospital, Hare was given a paper with an address on it, an address in an older part of the city where he had used to go often, to look at buildings.

It was strange to be once again alone on the street. Not often in the last months had he been alone at all, and never on the street. Except that a thin rain was falling, cold and hastening, he might have wandered for a while through the squares and alleys of the quarter; they seemed at once new and familiar to him, and the sensation of walking there was both vivifying and sad: the mixture of emotions made him feel painfully alive, and he wondered how long it would persist. But he turned up his collar and went on to the building to which he had been sent.

It was an old one, and one he remembered. He had stood before it more than once, feeling with his sight and his sense of proportion the curves of its stonework and its iron window-grilles. He had used to look in through the barred glass doors, down a long marble-floored hall bordered by columns, but he had never dared to go in. He went in now. There was an aged doorkeeper who took Hare's paper, made a remark about the rain and shuddered as though it were he who was wet and not Hare, and entered something on the terminal before him. He waited for a reply in the display, and when he had it, he left the little cage or box that was his station and led Hare down the long hall, past the columns pinkish and blue-veined like the legs of old people, to a tall open door. He waited for Hare to enter, then closed the door behind him.

The big room was empty. There was only a work station —a desk and two chairs, a terminal, a pile of printouts and other papers—which stood in the center of the floor, or not quite in the center, as though whoever had placed them there hadn't known that the room had a center. It did, though: it was clearly marked by the radiating diamonds of the parquet floor; it was plumb with the central diamond-shaped pendant of the chandelier, a multitiered forest of swagged lights and what seemed to be strings of jewels, that hung from the center of the ceiling above. Hare looked up at it as he crossed the floor to the desk; it swung around its axis, or rather seemed to swing, as he moved. He sat down in the chair beside the desk, crossed his hands in his lap, and waited. He didn't know who it was he waited for, or what disposition would be made of him now; he only supposed, with a sort of automatic humility he hardly even recognized in himself any longer, that whomever he waited for would be wiser than himself, would be able to see him clearly and know what was best.

That was one thing he had come to learn, over the last months—not how wise others were, but how unwise he was himself. He had learned to trust those who trusted in the world in a way that he could not: that way he hoped he might once again come to trust in the world himself. And even if he could not—even if there remained in him always some fatal mistrust—still there was no better thing that he could do: nothing else at all that he could do.

It hadn't been easy, learning that.

In the first weeks of his stay in the hospital, he had mostly been aware of the difference between himself and others, both those in difficulties like himself, and those attempting to help them. It seemed to him important, desperately important, to make those differences clear: to explain what it was in him that made him unlike others and unable to be as they were. It frightened him to be among so many who were bewildered, hurt, angry, or sad, not because he was not all these things himself, but because he felt himself to be unimaginable to them; and it frightened him more to be with the staff, because he could not define for them, in any way that he felt they could truly grasp, the perplexities within himself that made him unlike them: made him unwise, unwhole, divided and in pain, as they were not.

They were not even cadre for the most part, the staff, not anyway in the wing to which Hare was moved after a series of tests had determined there were no metabolic disorders at the root of his condition. (He had briefly hoped that some such disorder would be discovered, to relieve him of the awful burden of finding the explanation elsewhere. But there was

none.) In his wing were those whose troubles were unanalyz-
able, and the staff there were only kind, only experienced and
sympathetic, only set to watch the disorders take their course,
and give what common help they could. And how could Hare
explain to them—heavy women who nodded and patted his
hand, male nurses who spoke in banalities—about act-field
theory, its unchallengeable truth, its danger to him?

He knew so much. In his long, long silences his own
explanations were his only occupation, and seemed to him all
that sustained him over an abyss. He knew, with great preci-
sion, what stood between him and happiness; he knew quite
well that he did not need to feel as he did, that just beyond his
feelings, just past his really quite simple and explainable error,
lay the real world, which he could reach if he could only stop
making this error, or even stop explaining the error to himself:
but when he tried to say these things aloud, to explain this
predicament to the nurses and the staff or the other patients,
the explanations hurt him; and the real world, as he talked,
grew more fearsomely remote.

The explanations broke, in the end, like a fever. Then
there were tears, and shameful incontinence of grief, and
helplessness; no help at all but kindness and attention, the
help of those who knew how little help they could be.

He had not believed it was possible to fall out of the
universe: yet he had experienced exactly that. He had fallen
out of the universe into explanations of why he could not fall
out of the universe. And he had to reach for the hands of
those who could not even envisage such a thing and be drawn
back in. In the common-rooms, with their old furniture worn
and stained as though by the sorrows of those who used it; in
the kitchens, where he clumsily helped with meals; in the
winter yards and the crossing paths of the grounds, he would
be swept by waves of healing integration, unwilled, as though
some severed part of him were drawing back within him:

waves of feeling that left him weak and still afraid of the strange things he contained. When those diminished, too, like the terrible explanations, then he was empty. He looked around himself at the world and knew that though he did not know it, it knew him. He ate its nourishing breakfasts, blinked in its watery winter sunlight, joined its talk tentatively, washed its dishes with humility. He could not fall out of it.

Willy, who had visited him weekly, bringing good food and (what Hare hungered more for) stories of the people Willy knew, came on a spring day to take him away. In his dossier, encoded now with thousands of others in the hospital's records, the course of his illness and its resolution were charted, he knew; and when the magnitude of his difference from others was accounted for, his absolute otherness factored in, they were exactly as act-field theory predicted. It was all right.

All right. He sat, hands folded in his lap, waiting beneath the chandelier.

When a dark woman in Blue of about his own age came through the far double doors, Hare stood. The woman waved to him apologetically across the vast room, picking up a folder from a cart of them by the door; smiling, she crossed the geometrical floor to where Hare stood.

Among cadre there was no rank, and therefore no marks of rank beyond the simple clothes of Blue they all wore. But subtle distinguishing marks had nevertheless arisen; Hare knew that the cluster of pens in this woman's pocket meant heavy responsibilities. There was more, though. In the last months the faces of those he met were often charged for him with intense but imaginary familiarity; and yet about this woman he was sure.

"I know you," he said.

She raised her eyebrows. She didn't know him.

"Yes," Hare said. "Years ago." He named the study

camp where in the summer of Hare's seventeenth year they had known one another, studied together, hiked together. As he spoke, he remembered the summer darkness of the common-room where late at night they had talked.

"Oh, yes," she said. "Yes, yes, I remember now. A long time ago." She smiled, remembering. "A long time."

She had opened Hare's dossier, and now drew out the drawings of buildings and the calculations of their geometries that Hare had made. The last time Hare had seen them was when he stood before the committee: so long ago.

"Do you know why you do this?" she asked. "Copy these things?"

"No. I like them, I like to look at such places, old places, and wonder how they came to be; what the people thought and felt who built them."

"History," she suggested. "The past."

"Yes."

"That interests us, too," she said. "My project, I mean."

"Oh," said Hare, not knowing what else to say. "Is yours . . . is it an Applications project?"

She smiled. "No," she said.

"Oh."

She rested her cheek again in the palm of her hand. "I think," she said, "that long ago there was another time like this one, when people lived in places whose history they didn't know, whose history they had forgotten. They had lost history because they knew so little. They called that ignorance 'darkness,' and when they began to relearn history, they called that knowledge 'light.' But we're in darkness, too. Not because we know so little, but because we know so much. It's not different."

"Knowing everything is not different from knowing nothing," Hare said. "Is that what you mean?"

She quoted an old principle of act theorists, one that had

become an adage of Revolutionary cadre: "We seek no solution—only knowledge of the problem."

She turned to the drawing of the building opposite the cathedral, whose lettering Hare had copied out. Her finger touched the words.

"Do you know what they mean?" Hare asked her.

"No," she said. She folded her hands before her. "When you went out to do these things . . ."

"It was always on my own time," Hare said. "On free days."

"Did you tell anyone where you were going, what you were doing?"

"Not usually. Not all of it." Hare stared down at the hat he held in his hands. He felt, like an old secret wound, his taste for history, like a peasant child's taste for eating dirt.

"It must have seemed," she said, "that you were leading a double life. Did you feel that way? That you were leading a double life?"

At her words hot tears rose to Hare's eyes with awful quickness, and he felt for a moment that he would sob, as he had sobbed so often at just such small remarks that winter. A double life: a life inside, and another outside, between which Hare was pulled apart.

"Will you go on doing this, now?" the woman asked gently, her eyes watching Hare's evident distress.

"I don't know," he said. He looked up. "I want to help," he said. "I want to do useful work. I know that I haven't been much help for a long time, but I'm stronger now. I want to be of use."

She turned over the picture, and pushed the pile toward Hare. For a moment he didn't understand that she was giving them back to him. "I think your project made a mistake when they removed you from the work you'd been doing," she said.

"You do?"

"I think the better thing would have been to release you from cadre altogether." She rested her cheek again in the palm of her hand. "What do you think?"

A storm of shame arose within Hare, a storm that made the dreadful imploding roar he had first heard in the truck returning from the country. It broke so quickly over him that he had to suppose he had all along been expecting precisely these words to be said to him. Through its great noise he could not hear his own answer: "I'll do as you think best," he said. "Whatever you think."

"Go to the people," the woman said.

Hare covered his eyes. "I'm not good for much," he said. "There's not much I know how to do."

"What I suggest is this," the woman said. "You'll get a ration card and find a place in the city. Then—go on with what you did. I mean the drawings and the investigations you liked. History."

Hare listened.

"If you would," she said, "I would like you to come back here, now and then, and talk to me—to my project—about what you are doing."

"That would be all right?" Hare said. "I could do that?"

"You can do as you like," she said. "You can go back to your project, too."

"No," Hare said, feeling a strange warmth at his breastbone. "No. I'll do as you say."

"I don't know what we can learn, but I think . . . well." Her humorous eyes regarded him steadily. "Anyway there's probably nothing better for you to do. You are an oddity, aren't you?"

"Yes," Hare said.

"Did you think the Revolution was not large enough to contain you?"

"No," Hare said, "I didn't think so." But he had: he understood at that moment that he had thought exactly that.

She took a card from his dossier and handed it to him. "Take this to Applications, in the old cathedral," she said. "They'll tell you what to do. Come back here when you like. I'll be glad to see you."

She stood; Hare's interview was evidently at an end. He twisted the hat he held in his hands.

"I was remembering," he said, "something you told me. That summer, when we met at study camp." He felt his heart fill with a familiar apprehension. "You said . . . We were talking about act-field theory, which I was working on then, and you told me you believed that there was no such thing really as act-field theory at all; but that so long as everybody believed there was such a theory, and cadre believed that it worked, then it *did* work."

"Yes?"

"Yes." Dreadful as the danger Hare felt himself to be in, narrow as the ledge he stood on, he had to ask: "Do you still think that?"

"No," she said. Her smile hadn't passed, but it had changed, as though she not only shared a memory with Hare, but a joke as well; or a secret. "No, I don't."

□

Hare walked through the old quarter of the city, not feeling the thin rain soaking through his shoes. He seemed to himself to be naked but warm, to be already not in Blue, and walking in the world for the first time, as though his feet created it step by step: the world he had fallen out of, the world into which Eva and Boy had gone. He laughed, in fear and hunger for it.

His desire was not what he had thought it to be: his desire for history, for Eva, for Boy, none of it was what he thought it was. He knew nothing, nothing of the world he walked in; but he might learn.

What a strange, what a foolish error for him to have made, Hare thought. If he were called again before the local committee to make restitution for the trouble he had caused, he could tell them: he had come, without knowing it, to see the world in hierarchies. He, with his years of training, his excellent education, had built hierarchies in his heart. He had not known it until he had been asked to resign from cadre and had been overcome with shame: as though to be in Blue were better than to be not in Blue, to be cadre better than to be among the people.

He had believed act-field theory governed the act-field, and not the reverse. But the act-field governed. In the computers of the Revolution, as in the corridors and hollows of Hare's heart and mind, there was only a virtuality, after all; a virtual real-world, and not a whole one. He was inside the act-field and not it inside him; so was the Revolution, and all its work.

"Oh, I see," he said aloud. He had stopped walking. At the end of the street the great square opened, crossed by a single person on foot, a single bicycle. The obscure huge buildings that bordered it were soft in the misty rain. Hare, for the first time, yet not as though for the first time, but as though coming to remember some commonplace thing of enormous, of vital, importance, saw the act-field. Still; calm; with no face, not kind, not cruel, not anything. He reached out with his mind to touch it, but everywhere he touched it, it parted, showing him spaces, interstices, emptinesses formed by the edge of himself facing the sparkling edge of the world.

Hare cried out, as though stung. He felt the sensation of an answer, a sensation like a physical shock. The answer was an answer to a figure-ground problem, the simplest figure-ground problem, a problem solved long ago. The answer was an emptiness, formed by the edges of two questions: but the sensation of the answer was like a bit of light, a point of light lit, flaring fiercely and burning out: a physical sensation, a brief coincidence, an act.

Then it was gone. Hare set out across the square.

NOVELTY

Novelty

I

HE FOUND, QUITE SUDDENLY AND JUST AS HE TOOK a stool midway down the bar, that he had been vouchsafed a theme. A notion about the nature of things that he had been turning over in his mind for some time had become, without his ever choosing it, the theme of a book. It had "fallen into place," as it's put, like the tumblers of a lock that a safecracker listens to, and—so he experienced it —with the same small, smooth sound.

The theme was the contrary pull men feel between Novelty and Security. Between boredom and adventure, between safety and dislocation, between the snug and the wild. Yes! Not only a grand human theme, but a truly *mammalian* theme, perhaps the only one. Curiosity killed the cat, we are warned, and warned with good reason, and yet we are curious. Cats could be a motif: cats asleep, taking their ease in that superlatively comfortable way they have—you feel drowsy and snug just watching them. Cats on the prowl, endlessly prying. Cats tiptoe-walking away from fearsome novelty, hair on fire and faces shocked. He chuckled, pleased with this, and lifted the glass that had been set before him. From the great window south light poured through the golden liquor, refracted delicately by ice.

N O V E L T Y

The whole high front of the Seventh Saint Bar & Grill where he sat is of glass, floor to ceiling, a glass divided by vertical beams into a triptych and deeply tinted brown. During the day nothing of the dimly lit interior of the bar can be seen from the outside; walkers-by see only themselves, darkly; often they stop to adjust their clothing or their hair in what seems to them to be a mirror, or simply gaze at themselves in passing, momentarily but utterly absorbed, unaware that they are caught at it by watchers inside. (Or watcher, today, he being so far the bar's sole customer.) Seen from inside the bar, the avenue, the stores opposite, the street glimpsed going off at right angles, the trapezoid of sky visible above the lower buildings, are altered by the tinted windows into an elsewhere, oddly peaceful, a desert or the interior of the sea. Sometimes when he has fallen asleep face upward in the sun, his dreams have taken on this quality of supernatural bright darkness.

Novelty. Security. *Novelty* wouldn't be a bad title. It had the grandness of abstraction, alerting the reader that large and thoughtful things were to be bodied forth. As yet he had no inkling of any incidents or characters that might occupy his theme; perhaps he never would. He could see though the book itself, he could feel its closed heft and see it opened, white pages comfortably large and shadowed gray by print; dense, numbered, full of meat. He sensed a narrative voice, speaking calmly and precisely, with immense assurance building, building; a voice too far off for him to hear, but speaking.

The door of the bar opened, showing him a momentary oblong of true daylight, blankly white. A woman entered. He couldn't see her face as she crossed to the bar in front of the window, but he could see, drawn with exactitude by the light behind her, her legs within a summery white dress. When young he had supposed, without giving it much thought, that women didn't realize that sun behind them revealed them in this way; now he supposes that of course they must, and thinks about it.

"Well, look who's here," said the bartender. "You off today?"

"I took off," she said, and as she took a seat between him and the window, he saw that she was known to him, that is, they had sat here in this relation before. "I couldn't stand it anymore. What's tall and cool and not too alcoholic?"

"How about a spritzer?"

"Okay."

He caught himself staring fixedly at her, trying to remember if they had spoken before, and she caught him, too, raising her eyes to him as she lifted the pale drink to her lips, large dark eyes with startling whites; and looked away again quickly.

Where was he again? Novelty, security. He felt the feet of his attention skate out from under him in opposite directions. Should he make a note? He felt for the smooth shape of his pen in his pocket. "Theme for a novel: The contrary pull . . ." No. If this notion were real, he needn't make a note. A notion on which a note had to be made would be stillborn anyway, his notebook was a parish register of such, born and dead on the same page. Let it live if it can.

But had he spoken to her before? What had he said?

I I

When he was in college, a famous poet made a useful distinction for him. He had drunk enough in the poet's company to be compelled to describe to him a poem he was thinking of. It would be a monologue of sorts, the self-contemplation of a student on a summer afternoon who is reading

NOVELTY

Euphues. The poem itself would be a subtle series of euphuisms, translating the heat, the day, the student's concerns, into symmetrical posies; translating even his contempt and boredom with that famously foolish book into a euphuism.

The poet nodded his big head in a sympathetic, rhythmic way as this was explained to him, then told him that there are two kinds of poems. There is the kind you write; there is the kind you talk about in bars. Both kinds have value and both are poems; but it's fatal to confuse them.

In the Seventh Saint, many years later, it had struck him that the difference between himself and Shakespeare wasn't talent—not especially—but *nerve.* The capacity not to be frightened by his largest and most potent conceptions, to simply (simply!) sit down and execute them. The dreadful lassitude he felt when something really large and multifarious came suddenly clear to him, something *Lear*-sized yet sonnet-precise. If only they didn't rush on him whole, all at once, massive and perfect, leaving him frightened and nerveless at the prospect of articulating them word by scene by page. He would try to believe they were of the kind told in bars, not the kind to be written, though there was no way to be sure of this except to attempt the writing; he would raise a finger (the novelist in the bar mirror raising the obverse finger) and push forward his change. Wailing like a neglected ghost, the vast notion would beat its wings into the void.

Sometimes it would pursue him for days and years as he fled desperately. Sometimes he would turn to face it, and do battle. Once, twice, he had been victorious, objectively at least. Out of an immense concatenation of feeling, thought, word, and transcendent meaning had come his first novel, a slim, silent pageant of a book, tombstone for his slain conception. A publisher had taken it, gingerly; had slipped it quietly into the deep pool of spring releases, where it sank without a ripple, and where he supposes it lies still, its calm Bodoni gone long since green. A second, just as slim but more lurid, night-marish even, about imaginary murders in an imaginary exotic locale, had been sold for a movie, though the movie had never been made. He felt guilt for the producer's failure (which perhaps the producer didn't feel), having known the book could not be filmed; he had made a large sum, enough to finance years of this kind of thing, on a book whose first printing was largely returned.

His editor now and then took him to an encouraging lunch, and talked about royalties, advances, and upcoming titles, letting him know that whatever doubts he had she considered him a member of the profession, and deserving of a share in its largesse and its gossip; at their last one, some months before, she had pressed him for a new book, some-thing more easily graspable than his others. "A couple of chapters, and an outline," she said. "I could tell from that."

Well, he *was* sort of thinking of something, but it wasn't really shaping up, or rather it was shaping up rather like the others, into something indescribable at bottom. . . . "What it would be," he said timidly, "would be sort of a Catholic novel, about growing up Catholic," and she looked warily up at him over her Campari.

The first inkling of this notion had come to him the Christ-mas before, at his daughter's place in Vermont. On Christmas Eve, as indifferent evening took hold in the blue squares of the windows, he sat alone in the crepuscular kitchen, imbued with a profound sense of the identity of winter and twilight, of twilight and time, of time and memory, of his childhood and that Church which on this night waited to celebrate the sec-ond greatest of its feasts. For a moment or an hour as he sat, become one with the blue of the snow and the silence, a congruity of star, cradle, winter, sacrament, self, it was as though he listened to a voice that had long been trying to catch his attention, to tell him, Yes, this was the subject long withheld from him, which he now knew, and must eventually act on.

He had managed, though, to avoid it. He only brought it out now to please his editor, at the same time aware that it wasn't what she had in mind at all. But he couldn't do better; he had really only the one subject, if subject was the word for it, this idea of a notion or a holy thing growing clear in the stream of time, being made manifest in unexpected ways to an assortment of people: the revelation itself wasn't important, it could be anything, almost. Beyond that he had only one interest, the seasons, which he could describe endlessly and with all the passion of a country-bred boy grown old in the city. He was coming to doubt (he said) whether these were sufficient to make any more novels out of, though he knew that writers of genius had made great ones out of less. He supposed really (he didn't say) that he wasn't a novelist at all, but a failed poet, like a failed priest, one who had perceived that in fact he had no vocation, had renounced his vows, and yet had found nothing at all else in the world worth doing when measured by the calling he didn't have, and went on through life fatally attracted to whatever of the sacerdotal he could find or invent in whatever occupation he fell into, plumbing or psychiatry or tending bar.

I I I

"Boring, boring, *boring,*" said the woman down the bar from him. "I feel like taking off for good." Victor, the bartender, chin in his hand and elbow on the bar, looked at her with the remote sympathy of confessors and bartenders.

"Just take off," she said.

"So take off," Victor said. "Jeez, there's a whole world out there."

She made a small noise to indicate she doubted there was. Her brilliant eyes, roving over her prospects, fell on his where they were reflected in the bar mirror. She gazed at him but (he knew) didn't see him, for she was looking within. When she did shift focus and understand she was being regarded, she smiled briefly and glanced at his real person, then bent to her drink again. He summoned the bartender.

"Another, please, Victor."

"How's the writing coming?"

"Slowly. Very slowly. I just now thought of a new one, though."

"Izzat so."

It was so; but even as he said it, as the stirring-stick he had just raised out of his glass dripped whiskey drop by drop back into it, the older notion, the notion he had been unable at all adequately to describe to his editor, which he had long since dropped or thought he had dropped, stirred within him. Stirred mightily, though he tried to shut doors on it; stirred, rising, and came forth suddenly in all the panoply with which he had forgotten it had come to be dressed, its facets glittering, windows opening on vistas, great draperies billowing. It seemed to have grown old in its seclusion but more potent, and fiercely reproachful of his neglect. Alarmed, he tried to shelter his tender new notion of Novelty and Security from its onrush, but even as he attempted this, the old notion seized upon the new, and as he watched helplessly, the two coupled in an utter ravishment and interlacement, made for each other, one thing now and more than twice as compelling as each had been before. "Jesus," he said aloud; and then looked up, wondering if he had been heard. Victor and the woman were tête-à-tête, talking urgently in undertones.

I V

"I know, I know," he'd said, raising a hand to forestall his editor's objection. "The Catholic Church is a joke. Especially the Catholic Church I grew up in . . ."

"Sometimes a grim joke."

"And it's been told a lot. The nuns, the weird rules, all that decayed scholastic guff. The prescriptions, and the pro-scriptions—especially the proscriptions, all so trivial when they weren't hurtful or just ludicrous. But that's not the way it's perceived. For a kid, for me, the Church organized the whole world—not morally, either, or not especially, but in its whole nature. Even if the kid isn't particularly moved by thoughts of God and sin—I wasn't—there's still a lot of Church left over, do you see? Because all the important things about the Church were real things: objects, places, words, sights, smells, days. The liturgical calendar. The Eastern church must be even more so. For me, the Church was mostly about the seasons: it kept them in order. The Church was coextensive with the world."

"So the kid's point of view against—"

"No, no. What I would do, see, to get around this contra-diction between the real Church and this other church I seemed to experience physically and emotionally, is to reimagine the Catholic Church as another kind of church altogether, a very subtle and wise church, that understood all these feelings; a church that was really—secretly—*about* these things in fact, and not what it seemed to be about; and then pretend, in the book, that the church I grew up in was that church."

"You're going to invent a whole new religion?"

"Well, not exactly. It would just be a matter of shifting

emphasis, somehow, turning a thing a hundred and eighty degrees . . .''

"Well, how? Do you mean 'books in the running brooks, sermons in stones,' that kind of thing? Pantheism?"

"No. No. The opposite. In that kind of religion the trees and the sky and the weather *stand for* God or some kind of supernatural unity. In my religion, God and all the rituals and sacraments would stand for the real world. The religion would be a means of perceiving the real world in a sacramental way. A Gnostic ascension. A secret at the heart of it. And the secret is—everything. Common reality. The day outside the church window."

"Hm."

"That's what it would really have been about from the beginning. And only seemed to be about these divine person- ages, and stuff, and these rules."

She nodded slowly in a way that showed she followed him but frankly saw no novel. He went on, wanting at least to say it all before he no longer saw it with this clarity. "The priests and nuns would know this was the case, the wisest of them, and would guide the worshipers—the ones they thought could grasp it—to see through the paradox, to see that it *is* a paradox: that only by believing, wholly and deeply, in all of it could you see through it one day to what is real— see through Christmas to the snow; see through the fasting, and the saints' lives, and the sins, and Baby Jesus walking through the snow every Christmas night ringing a little bell—"

"What?"

"That was a story one nun told. That was a thing she said was the case."

"Good heavens. Did she believe it?"

"Who knows? That's what I'm getting at."

She broke into her eggs Florentine with a delicate fork. The two chapters, full of meat; the spinach of an outline. She was very attractive in a coltish, aristocratic way, with a *framboise* flush on her tanned cheeks that was just the flush his wife's cheeks had had. No doubt still had; no doubt.

"Like Zen," he said desperately. "As though it were a kind of Zen."

V

Well, he had known as well as she that it was no novel, no matter that it importuned him, reminding him often of its deep truth to his experience, and suggesting shyly how much fun it might be to manipulate, what false histories he could invent that would account for the Church he imagined. But he had it now; now the world began to turn beneath him firmly, both rotating and revolving; it was quite clear now.

The *theme* would not be religion at all, but this ancient conflict between Novelty and Security. This theme would be embodied in the contrasted adventures of a set of *characters,* a family of Catholic believers modeled on his own. The *motion* of the book would be the sense of a holy thing ripening in the stream of time, that is, the seasons; and the *form* would be a false history or mirror-reversal of the world he had known and the Church he had believed in.

Absurdly, his heart had begun to beat fast. Not years from now, not months, very soon, imaginably soon, he could begin. That there was still nothing concrete in what he envisioned didn't bother him, for he was sure this scheme was one that would generate concreteness spontaneously and easily. He had planted a banner amid his memories and imaginings, a banner to which they could all repair, to which they were repairing even now, primitive clans vivified by these colors, clamoring to be marshaled into troops by the captains of his art.

It would take a paragraph, a page, to eliminate, say, the

Reformation, and thus make his Church infinitely more aged, bloated, old in power, forgetful of dogmas long grown universal and ignorable, dogmas altered by subtle subversives into their opposites, by a brotherhood within the enormous bureaucracy of faith, a brotherhood animated by a holy irony and secret as the Rosicrucians. Or contrariwise: he could pretend that the Reformation had been more nearly a complete success than it was, leaving his Roman faith a small, inward-turning, Gnostic sect, poor and not grand, guiltless of the Inquisition; its Pope itinerant or in shabby exile somewhere (Douai, or Alexandria, or Albany); through Appalachia a poor priest travels from church to church, riding the circuit in an old Studebaker as rusty black as his cassock, putting up at a gaunt frame house on the outskirts of town, a convent. The wainscoted parlor is the nuns' chapel, and the pantry is full of their canning; in autumn the broken stalks of corn wither in their kitchen garden. "Use it up, wear it out," says the proverb of their creed (and not that of splendid and orgulous Protestants), "make it do, do without": and they possess themselves in edgeworn and threadbare Truth.

Yes! The little clapboard church in Kentucky where his family had worshiped, in the Depression, amid the bumptious Baptists. In the hastening dawn he had walked a mile to serve six o'clock mass there. In winter the stove's smell was incense; in summer it was the damp odor of morning coming through the lancet windows, opened a crack to reveal a band of blue-green day beneath the feet of the saints fragilely pictured there in imitation stained-glass. The three or four old Polish women always present always took Communion, their extended tongues trembling and their veined closed eyelids trembling, too; and though when they rose crossing themselves they became only unsanctified old women again, he had for a moment glimpsed their clean pink souls. There were aged and untended rose bushes on the sloping lawn of the big

gray house he had grown up in—his was by far the best off of
any family in that little parish—and when the roses bloomed
in May the priest came and the familiar few they saw in
church each week gathered, and the Virgin was crowned
there, a Virgin pink and blue and white as the rose-burdened
day, the best lace tablecloth beneath her, strange to see that
domestic lace outdoors edge-curled by odorous breezes and
walked on by bugs. He caught himself singing:

> O Mary, we crown thee with blossoms today
> Queen of the Angels
> Queen of the May

Of course he would lose by this scheme a thousand other
sorts of memories just as dear, would lose the grand and the
fatuous baroque, mitered bishops in jewel-encrusted copes
and steel-rimmed eyeglasses; but the point was not nostalgia
and self-indulgence after all, no, the opposite; in fact there
ought to be some way of tearing the heart completely out of
the old religion, or to conceive on it something so odd that no
reader would ever confuse it with the original, except that it
would be as concrete, its concreteness the same concreteness
(which was the point . . .) And what then had been that
religion's heart?

What if his Jesus hadn't saved mankind?

What if the Renaissance, besides uncovering the classical
past, had discovered evidence—manuscripts, documentary
proofs (incontrovertible, though only after terrible struggles)
—that Jesus had in the end refused to die on the cross? Had
run away; had abjured his Messiah-hood; and left his followers then to puzzle that out. It would not have been out of
cowardice, exactly, though the new New Testaments would
seem to say so, but (so the apologetic would come to run) out
of a desire to share our human life completely, even our

common unheroic fate. Because the true novelty, for God, would lie not in the redemption of men—an act he could perform with a millionth part of the creative effort he had expended in creating the world—but in being a human being entire, growing old and impotent to redeem anybody, including himself. Something like that had happened with the false messiah Sevi in the seventeenth century: his Messiah-hood spread quickly and widely through the whole Jewish world; then, at the last minute, threatened with death, he'd converted to Islam. His followers mostly fell away, but a few still believed, and their attempts to figure out how the Messiah could act in that strange way, redeem us by not redeeming us, yielded up the Hassidic sect, with its Kabbalah and its paradoxical parables, almost Zenlike; very much what he had in mind for his church.

"A man of sorrows, and acquainted with grief"—the greatest grief, far greater than a few moments' glorious pain on that Tree. Mary's idea of it was that in the end the Father was unable to permit the death of his only-begotten son; the prophecy is Abraham and Isaac; she interceded for him, of course, her son, too, as she still intercedes for each of us. Perhaps he resented it. In any case he outlived her, and his own wife and son, too; lived on, a retired carpenter, in his daughter's house; and the rabble came before his door, and they mocked him, saying: *If thou art the Christ, take up thy cross.*

Weird! But, but—what made him chuckle and nearly smack his lips (in full boil now)—the thing would be, that his characters would pursue their different destinies *completely oblivious of all this oddity,* oblivious, that is, that it *is* odd; the narrative voice wouldn't notice it either; their Resurrection has always been this ambiguous one, this Refusal; their holy-card of Jesus in despised old age (after Murillo) has always marked the Sundays in their missals; their Church is just the old, the homely, the stodgy great Security, Peter's rock, which his was. His priest would venture out (bored, restless) from that security into the strange and the dangerous, at first only wishing to be a true priest, then for their own sakes, for the adventure of understanding. A nun: starting from a wild embracing of all experience, anything goes, she passes later into quietness and, well, into habit. His wife would have to sit for that portrait, of course, of course; though she wouldn't sit still. The two meet after long separation, only to pass each other at the X-point, coming from different directions, headed for different heavens—a big scene there. A saint: but which one? He or she? Well, that had always been the question; neither, or both, or one seeing at last after the other's death his sainthood, and advocating it (in the glum Vatican, a Victorian pile in Albany, the distracted Pope), a miracle awaited and given at last, unexpectedly, or not given, withheld—oh, hold on, he asked, stop a minute, slow down. He plucked out and lit a cigarette with care. He placed his glass more exactly in the center of its cardboard coaster and arranged his change in orbits around it.

Flight over. Cats, though. He would appropriate for his Jesus that story about Muhammad called from his couch, tearing off his sleeve rather than disturbing the cat that had fallen asleep on it. A parable. Did Jews keep cats then? Who knows.

Oh God how subtle he would have to be, how cunning. . . . No paragraph, no phrase even of the thousands the book must contain could strike a discordant note, be less than fully imagined, an entire novel's worth of thought would have to be expended on each one. His attention had only to lapse for a moment, between preposition and object, colophon and chapter heading, for dead spots to appear like gangrene that would rot the whole. Silkworms didn't work as finely or as patiently as he must, and yet boldness was all, the large stroke, the end contained in and prophesied by the beginning, the stains of his clouds infinitely various but all signifying sunrise. Unity in diversity, all that guff. An enormous weariness flew over him. The trouble with drink, he had long known, wasn't that it started up these large things but that it belittled the awful difficulties of their execution. He drank, and gazed out into the false golden day, where a passage of girl students in plaid uniforms was just then occurring, passing secret glances through the trick mirror of the window.

V I

"I'm such a chicken," the woman said to Victor. "The other day they were going around at work signing people up for the softball team. I really wanted to play. They said come on, come on, it's no big deal, it's not professional or anything . . ."

"Sure, just fun."

"I didn't dare."

"What's to dare? Just good exercise. Fresh air."

"Sure, *you* can say that. You've probably been playing all your life." She stabbed at the last of her ice with a stirring-stick. "I really wanted to, too. I'm such a chicken."

Play right field, he wanted to advise her. That had always been his retreat, nothing much ever happens in right field, you're safe there mostly unless a left-handed batter gets up, and then if you blow one, the shame is quickly forgotten. He told himself to say to her: *You should have volunteered for right field.* But his throat said it might refuse to do this, and his pleasantry could come out a muffled croak, watch out. She had finished her drink; how much time did he have to think of a thing to say to her? Buy her a drink: the sudden offer always made him feel like a masher, a cad, something antique and repellent.

"You should have volunteered for right field," he said.

"Oh, hi," she said. "How's the writing coming?"

"What?"

"The last time we talked you were writing a novel."

"Oh. Well, I sort of go in spurts." He couldn't remember still that he had ever talked with her, much less what imaginary novel he had claimed to be writing.

"It's like coming into a cave here," she said, raising her glass, empty now except for the rounded remains of ice. "You can't see anything for a while. Because of the sun in your eyes. I didn't recognize you at first." The ice she wanted couldn't escape from the bottom of the glass till she shook the glass briskly to free it; she slid a piece into her mouth then and crunched it heedlessly (a long time since he'd been able to do that) and drew her skirt away from the stool beside her, which he had come to occupy.

"Will you have another?"

"No, nope." They smiled at each other, each ready to go on with this if the other could think of something to go on with.

"So," he said.

"Taking a break?" she said. "Do you write every day?"

"Oh, no. Oh, I sort of try. I don't work very hard, really. Really I'm on vacation. All the time. Or you could say I work all the time, too. It comes to the same thing." He'd said all this before, to others; he wondered if he'd said it to her. "It's like weekend homework. Remember? There wasn't ever a time you absolutely had to do it—there was always Saturday, then Sunday—but then there wasn't ever a time when it wasn't there to do, too."

"How awful."

Sunday dinner's rich odor declining into stale leftoverhood: was it that incense that made Sunday Sunday, or what? For there was no part of Sunday that was not Sunday;

even if, rebelling, you changed from Sunday suit to Saturday jeans when dinner was over, they felt not like a second skin, like a bold animal's useful hide, as they had the day before, but strange, all right but wrong to flesh chafed by wool, the flannel shirt too smooth, too indulgent after the starched white. And upstairs—though you kept as far from them as possible, that is, facedown and full-length on the parlor carpet, head inches from the funnies—the books and blue-lined paper waited.

"It must take a lot of self-discipline," she said.

"Oh, I don't know. I don't have much." He felt himself about to say again, and unable to resist saying, that "Dumas, I think it was Dumas, some terrifically prolific Frenchman, said that writing novels is a simple matter—if you write one page a day, you'll write one novel a year; two pages a day, two novels a year; three pages, three novels, and so on. And how long does it take to cover a page with writing? Twenty minutes? An hour? So you see. Very easy really."

"I don't know," she said, laughing. "I can't even bring myself to write a letter."

"Oh, now *that's* hard." Easiest to leave it all just as it had been, and only inveigle into it a small sect of his own making . . . easiest of all just to leave it. It was draining from him, like the suits of the bathing beauties pictured on trick tumblers, to opposite effect. Self-indulgence only, nostalgia, pain of loss for what had not ever been worth saving: the self-indulgence of a man come to that time when the poignance of memory is his sharpest sensation, grown sharp as the others have grown blunt. The journey now quite obviously more than half over, it had begun to lose interest; only the road already traveled still seemed full of promise. Promise! Odd word. But there it was. He blinked, and having fallen rudely silent, said, "Well, well, well."

"Well," she said. She had begun to gather up the small

habitation she had made before her on the bar, purse and open wallet, folded newspaper, a single unblown rose he hadn't noticed her bring in. "I'd like to read your book sometime."

"Sure," he said. "It's not very good. I mean, it has some nice things in it, it's a good little story. But it's nothing really."

"I'm sure it's terrific." She spun the rose beneath her nose and alighted from her stool.

"I happen to have a lot of copies. I'll give you one."

"Good. Got to go."

On her way past him she gave the rose to Victor without any other farewell. Once again sun described her long legs as she crossed the floor (sun lay on its boards like gilding, sun was impartial), and for a moment she paused, sun-blinded maybe, in the garish lozenge of real daylight made when she opened the door. Then she reappeared in the other afternoon of the window. She raised her hand in a command, and a cab the color of marigolds appeared before her as though conjured. A flight of pigeons filled up the window all in an instant, seeming stationary there like a sculpted frieze, and then just as instantly didn't fill it up anymore.

"Crazy," Victor said.

"Hm?"

"Crazy broad." He gestured with the rose toward the vacant window. "My wife. You married?"

"I was. Like the pumpkin eater." Handsome guy, Victor, in a brutal, black-Irish way. Like most New York bartenders, he was really an actor, or was it the reverse?

"Divorced?"

"Separated."

He tested his thumb against the pricks of the rose. "Women. They say you got all the freedom. Then you give them their freedom, and they don't want it."

He nodded, though it wasn't wisdom that his own case

would have yielded up. He was only glad now not to miss her any longer; and now and then, sad that he was glad. The last precipitate was that occasionally when a woman he'd been looking at, on a bus, in a bar, got up to leave, passing away from him for good, he felt a shooting pang of loss absurd on the face of it.

Volunteer, he thought, but for right field. And if standing there you fall into a reverie, and the game in effect goes on without you, well, you knew it would when you volunteered for the position. Only once every few innings the lost—the not-even-noticed-till-too-late—fly ball makes you sorry that things are as they are and not different, and you wonder if people think you might be bored and indifferent out there, contemptuous even, which isn't the case at all. . . .

"On the house," Victor said, and rapped his knuckles lightly on the bar.

"Oh, hey, thanks." Kind Victor, though the glass put before him contained a powerful solvent, he knew that even as he raised the glass to his lips. He could still fly, oh yes, always, though the cost would be terrible. But what was it he fled from? Self-indulgence, memory dearer to him than any adventure, solitude, lapidary work in his very own mines . . . what could be less novel, more secure? And yet it seemed dangerous; it seemed he hadn't the nerve to face it; he felt unarmed against it.

Novelty and Security: the security of novelty, the novelty of security. Always the full thing, the whole subject, the *true* subject, stood just behind the one you found yourself contemplating. The trick, but it wasn't a trick, was to take up at once the thing you saw and the reason you saw it as well; to always bite off more than you could chew, and then chew it. If it were self-indulgence for him to cut and polish his semiprecious memories, and yet seem like danger, like a struggle he was unfit for, then self-indulgence was a potent force, he must examine it, he must reckon with it.

And he would reckon with it: on that last Sunday in Advent, when his story was all told, the miracle granted or refused, the boy would lift his head from the books and blue-lined paper, the questions that had been set for him answered, and see that it had begun to snow.

Snow not falling but flying sidewise, and sudden, not signaled by the slow curdling of clouds all day and a flake or two drifting downward, but rushing forward all at once as though sent for. (The blizzard of '36 had looked like that.) And filling up the world's concavities, pillowing up in the gloaming, making night light with its whiteness, and then falling still in everyone's dreams, falling for pages and pages; steepling (so an old man would dream in his daughter's house) the gaunt frame convent on the edge of town, and drifting up even to the eyes of the martyrs pictured on the sash windows of the little clapboard church, Our Lady of the Valley; the wind full of howling white riders tearing the shingles from the roof, piling the snow still higher, blizzarding the church away entirely and the convent too and all the rest of it, so that by next day oblivion whiter than the hair of God would have returned the world to normality, covering his false history and all its works in the deep ordinariness of two feet of snow; and at evening the old man in his daughter's house would sit looking out over the silent calm alone at the kitchen table, a congruence of star, cradle, season, sacrament, etc., end of chapter thirty-five, the next page a flyleaf blank as snow.

The whole thing, the full thing, the step taken backward that frames the incomprehensible as in a window. *Novelty:* there was, he just then saw, a pun in the title.

He rose. Victor, lost in thought, watched the hurrying crowds that had suddenly filled the streets, afternoon gone, none with time to glance at themselves; hurrying home. One page a day, seven a week, thirty or thirty-one to the month. Fishing in his pocket for a tip, he came up with his pen, a thick black fountain pen. Fountain: it seemed less flowing, less forthcoming than that, in shape more like a bullet or a bomb.

ABOUT THE AUTHOR

Praised by Russell Hoban as "one of those necessary writers for whom one has been waiting without knowing it," John Crowley is the author of the World Fantasy Award-nominated *Ægypt,* as well as *The Deep, Beasts, Engine Summer,* and the World Fantasy Award-winning *Little, Big.* He currently lives in the Berkshire Hills of western Massachusetts.